UNTIL THE END

RICK WOOD

BLOOD SPLATTER PRESS

ABOUT THE AUTHOR

Rick Wood is a British writer born in Cheltenham.

His love for writing came at an early age, as did his battle with mental health. After defeating his demons, he grew up and became a stand-up comedian, then a drama and English teacher, before giving it all up to become a full-time author.

He now lives in Cheltenham, where he divides his time between watching horror, reading horror, and writing horror.

ALSO BY RICK WOOD

The Sensitives:

Book One – The Sensitives

Book Two – My Exorcism Killed Me

Book Three – Close to Death

Book Four – Demon's Daughter

Book Five – Questions for the Devil

Book Six - Repent

Book Seven - The Resurgence

Book Eight - Until the End

Shutter House

Shutter House

Prequel Book One - This Book is Full of Bodies

Cia Rose:

Book One – After the Devil Has Won

Book Two – After the End Has Begun

Book Three - After the Living Have Lost

Book Four - After the Dead Have Decayed

Chronicles of the Infected

Book One – Zombie Attack

Book Two – Zombie Defence

Book Three – Zombie World

Standalones:

When Liberty Dies

I Do Not Belong

Death of the Honeymoon

Sean Mallon:

Book One – The Art of Murder

Book Two – Redemption of the Hopeless

The Edward King Series:

Book One – I Have the Sight

Book Two – Descendant of Hell

Book Three – An Exorcist Possessed

Book Four – Blood of Hope

Book Five – The World Ends Tonight

Non-Fiction

How to Write an Awesome Novel

Thrillers published as Ed Grace:

The Jay Sullivan Thriller Series

Assassin Down

Kill Them Quickly

The Bars That Hold Me

MANY, MANY YEARS AGO

1

WHAT WAS ONCE A GRAND PIECE OF ARCHITECTURE, A CLASSIC Buddhist structure, had become a rejected mess of moss and weathered stone.

The roof that once provided shelter to this great monastery was coated in greenery — not greenery like a stunning forest landscape, or a beautiful orchard, but like vines and weeds and marshland. A tree that had once over-hung with natural beauty was now cracking the floor with its roots, its stumps crawling down tiles and walls like the splayed legs of a squid.

To Om Samsara, this structure was not the wreckage most believed it to be. It was not an abandoned wasteland, nor was it a deserted landmark left to rot.

It was the place he became a bhikkhu; it was his battle-ground and, should this work, it would be his home.

Mara was strong, but that was to be expected. A creature full of absolute evil was a most formidable opponent. He was the accumulation of all temptation, sin and death; the intrinsic and external burden of condemnation — he was the one who had tried to tempt Buddha himself, but was so fortunately rejected.

But Mara was relentless; he had spent so many years trying to find his way back to the world, trying to reject the balance of good and evil, trying to take Earth and replace it with Hell. Should he ever succeed, Om could only imagine the devastation that would occur.

That was why it was imperative that he defeated this entity, and the hatred that filled it

Om knew that everything was connected. Everything is because other things are. This links the beauty of the world; the forest, the trees, the feeling one would call love. But this was not limited to just the good in the world.

Understanding this was crucial to defeating Mara.

That was why this temple was his only hope. Knowing that Mara was coming, he had spent weeks protecting it, creating a sanctity, a protected ground. This temple was integral to any hope of winning.

He had waited for weeks, but he did not need to wait any longer. The time had come. He was ready.

Om stood in the temple's centre, bare feet beneath his robes, not bothered by the bumps of a broken stone floor. He had let go of pain, just as he had let go of possessions. He would take what came to him in this life with the belief that it's what's required to make it to the next.

The sun crept behind a cloud.

Shadows encompassed the temple's already darkened architecture.

The wind blew, but in no particular direction.

Om was ready for this moment. He had been studying for it, preparing for it; creating a holy ground that would provide him protection and strength.

He would not let himself be tempted. In that, he was determined.

Mara would attempt to divert Om from his mission. Mara would use anything he could that might entice Om to give up on his teachings, but Om was prepared for a big fight; for fire, for rage, for war. He'd prepared what he would say, and how he would handle it. He was ready for the vile beast to reveal itself and begin the fight.

Which was why he was so taken aback to see a woman's figure emerge, walking from the distant shade. The silhouette was familiar. It was from a long time ago, but he remembered tracing his hand across its outline, wishing he could do what he could not.

He had never allowed himself to verbalise his love for her, for that was something he was not allowed to do. Sure, he had been tempted, and she had begged him to stop denying what they had, but he had not given in.

She married years later, and he had let her go; just as he had let go of all possessions, all ties to this world, and anything else that may provoke greed. That's why he understood what this was.

A test.

Mara needed to tempt him into lust, to greed, in order to penetrate the darker sides of his being.

Om, however, just needed to stay strong.

Yet, as her face emerged, and she walked toward him, he wanted to throw everything away just for a moment with this apparition.

"Om," she said. "What are you doing?"

She was so inquisitive, so bemused. Like she was astounded that he was taking on this challenge, that he was even attempting to ward off Mara. Like he was betraying her by doing so.

But it was not her.

It was not Cahya.

Her name meant *one who is the light in the darkness.*

And that's what she was; only not to him.

She held out a hand. It touched his cheek, and it felt just like it had felt when he was young.

He refused to let it tempt him, but it was tough, too tough.

"You need to stop this," she whispered, her face sad, in pain.

"It's not you," Om said, but so quietly and with such little conviction that it meant nothing.

"You need to give in. You need to let Mara win, it's the only way we can be together."

"Stop."

"It's the only way—"

"Stop."

He pushed her back, held his hands out to keep her at arm's length, and glared.

"With every breath I take today," he began, "I vow to be awake."

He stepped toward her and pushed her back.

"And every step I take," he continued, "I vow to take with a grateful heart."

She backed away. Crying. Looking so lost.

"Om, what are you doing?"

"So I may see with eyes of love into the hearts of all I meet."

"Stop it, you're hurting me."

"To ease their burden when I can and touch them with a smile of peace."

She fell to her knees. Looking up at him.

Scowling.

"You're going to die, you know," she said, and then she was gone.

Om looked around. Waiting for the next obstacle Mara

would throw at him. The shadows remained, and wind was cold, but he was alone again.

Except he wasn't.

Only a fool would believe he was alone.

And, just outside the temple's edge, he saw it. Shining brightly.

Gold. Bright, shining gold. It must be worth millions, probably more.

Om laughed.

"Is that the best you can do?" he asked.

He stared determinedly into the darkness. He did not shout, he did not fret, and he did not back down.

This was exactly what Mara did. He tried to tempt you, tried to make you give in by providing you with what he believes you want. This was why it was so important Om listened to his teachings. He had no possessions that tied him to the physical world. He had let go of all love that had once attempted to destroy him. And he had removed himself of all fear, and for that reason, he was not even afraid of the epitome of evil itself.

A low growl echoed around the empty chambers. A rumble shook the ground, but he stood firm.

Mara was here.

"May I be a guard for those who need protection," he said, quietly, but knowing he was heard. "A guide for those on the path."

An orange cloud of fire approached, floating from the distance.

"A boat, a raft, a bridge for those who wish to cross the flood."

He stepped forward.

The cloud stopped at the edge of the temple. Hovered. Waited. Unable to come any closer.

Om smiled. This meant the weeks he had spent

protecting this ground had worked. He had created a fortress, a protection from Mara — meaning the only way Mara could defeat Om was to tempt him out of his sanctuary.

"May this be a lamp in the darkness, a resting place for the weary, a healing place for all who are sick, a vase of plenty, a tree of miracles."

He moved forward, stepping deliberately and carefully, until he reached the edge. He faced the amber glow of mist.

In the mist, there formed a face.

Om willed Mara to enter the temple, to come onto sacred ground, to fight him where Om could win.

But Mara never would. He would never enter a battle that he was doomed to lose. He would never risk failure — he had pride that could not stomach the fall.

They were at an impasse.

Om would not leave the template boundary, for fear of being defeated.

Mara would never enter the temple, for fear of not winning.

"May I bring sustenance and awakening, enduring like the earth and sky."

Om stepped backwards, retreating further into the temple, away from the face.

The face in the mist scowled.

It wanted Om to step out.

It wanted to kill him.

But Om would not be tempted.

And this was the moment; the precise moment when Om realised…

He was stuck. Through his own plan, he was stuck. Banished to this temple, never to leave. For, if he was to leave, Mara would take him. Hope would be lost.

Maybe he should just accept death and welcome it like an old friend.

But he had a feeling, a premonition if there was such a thing, that this ability to protect himself from evil, to put a guard up against The Devil, was a knowledge that no one else possessed.

He needed to keep that knowledge for the moment he had to pass it on.

So he would stay here and never leave.

"Until all beings are freed from sorrow."

He retreated further into the temple.

The face in the mist left. The clouds parted. The omen of malice dissipated.

"And all are awakened."

Om sat down to meditate in the forgotten temple that would now be his last and only home.

NOW

2

IT WAS AN UNSETTLING CALL THAT OSCAR HAD TO MAKE, YET he did not feel nervous.

In fact, he wasn't sure exactly what he felt anymore. Trepidation? Sadness? Resolve?

He had been fighting this fight for a while now. He often thought back to the moment it all went wrong, when he chose to rescue April and Julian, an action that meant the Sensitives temporarily abandoned this world and allowed the balance of good and evil to be shifted. He'd rescued the love of his life, knowing there would be devastating consequences. The unbalancing between Heaven and Hell, the disruption caused, had allowed Hell to open and spew its vile into this world. Mass demonic possession occurred on a scale too big for them to handle. Even Thea, who was a stronger Sensitive than all others and could even exorcise a building of demons at once, could not exorcise the entire world.

And what happens when a demon is not exorcised? Amalgamation incarnation. The process of the demon stealing its host's body completely, until they have taken their victim's place in this world. No exorcism would do anything then. And the world was close to being overrun by amalgamated victims.

Oscar had to be honest with himself, and with others. The war was lost. Hell had won. There was nothing they could do now.

And what if he had the chance to go back and rescue April again? Would he do anything differently?

Oscar wasn't sure. Possibly. Possibly not. Such a lack of ability to learn from his mistakes was probably why Julian had resented him so much.

Yet, despite how much he and Julian did not get on, he wouldn't mind a bit of guidance from him now. Unfortunately, he was an inevitable casualty of war.

And what good had rescuing April done? Her body was upstairs, writhing around on a bed, her wrists bound to the headboard, with the worst evil in the world inside of her.

The Devil.

Slowly eating away at her soul, using her to gain access to this world.

Oscar spent so much time ruminating about how it was his action that had brought the world to its knees. Every day on the news, more and more violence occurred. Hell was giving a push to mankind; a push that prompted people to commit the most horrendous acts. Children were killing their parents. People were starting wars. Good men and women were committing acts of atrocity.

No one understood why.

But Oscar did.

The sound of a Skype call ended his endless thoughts. He turned the laptop toward him and answered the call.

Father Lorenzo Romano appeared on his screen, a room from the Vatican behind him. Lorenzo was the man in charge of covering up the Sensitive's messes so the Church didn't have to answer difficult questions; the man who made sure no one knew what really happened in this world.

Imagine if people knew for sure that demonic forces were at work, and the chaos that would ensue...

Oscar hesitated. Lorenzo stared back. He did not want to be the one to break the silence, but it was going on too long, and someone needed to speak.

"You asked to speak to me," Lorenzo prompted.

Oscar could see Lorenzo was agitated. Everyone at the Church was angry with the Sensitives. Rightly so, Oscar decided. They had created this mess, and so far, they had failed to solve it.

"Yes," Oscar said, looking away from the screen. "Yes, I did."

"Well, what is it? Is there a problem with the recruits?"

Oscar sighed.

"I'm sending the recruits home," he answered. "They are leaving as we speak."

"You are *what*?"

"Lower your voice, Lorenzo, I don't appreciate being shouted at."

"How dare you! We send you these recruits, we find potential Sensitives, we scour the Earth for them, and you send them home?"

"It's pointless them being here. There's nothing they can do."

"Are you saying you have found a way of solving this situation without them?"

Oscar leant forward. Rubbed his sinus. Ran his hands over his face and through his hair.

The light above him shook. The ceiling rumbled.

It was awake.

"No," Oscar eventually replied. "I need you to pass on a message to the pope. To whoever needs to know."

"Oscar, I don't understand, what is this way you've found of solving it without–"

"Lorenzo, stop. There is no way of solving the situation."

"What are you saying?"

A clatter from above shook the ceiling again.

"The Devil is upstairs, tied to the bed. It is in April's body. It has found its way into this world, after all these years of trying, and… and, well, there's no way to stop it."

"What about Thea? Does she not–"

"Save yourself the time, for Christ's sake. It's done. It's over."

"I don't understand."

"We have lost. Hell has won. There is nothing more we can do."

Lorenzo stared. Said nothing. His mouth stuttered over a few syllables, clearly struggling to find the right words to say.

"That cannot be," Lorenzo said. "You are the Sensitives. We have given you everything you need. We have provided you with an army."

"An army of kids who can do very little against a world taken over by…"

Oscar stopped speaking. What was the point? He could explain this, be as succinct and simple with what he was saying, and Lorenzo would still not accept it. Lorenzo would expect them to go on fighting until the end.

Only Lorenzo didn't seem to realise. This was the end.

"This will be the last time I speak to you," Oscar said.

"You can't just say that they've won and–"

"Lorenzo, just… Go home. Be with your loved ones. Spend the last few weeks you have with those that you cherish most."

The ceiling clattered again.

"That's what I'll be doing," Oscar added.

"No, you can't just–"

"Goodbye, Lorenzo."

Oscar shut the laptop.

He sat there. Still. Listening to the pounding and screaming and banging from upstairs, knowing he would have to go up there soon.

He had a headache. He could have a cup of tea, as that always made him feel better — but what was the point?

There would not be anymore feeling better. Nor would there be any feeling worse.

There would be no feeling at all.

Soon, there would be nothing — and that would be the best-case scenario. The other possibility was that mankind was not given the fortune of death, but instead, Hell subjected them to an eternity of damnation and suffering.

The clatters grew louder.

He stood. He'd best go see how much of April was left.

3

A FEW DAYS AGO, THIS BUILDING WAS A HIVE OF FRESH recruits, bursting with potential. Students spoke excitedly about the opportunity they had to do good, about how they were finally understanding their abilities. There was a buzz, a feeling of anticipation.

Now there was a feeling of despair. Of grave resolve. Thea could see it in the faces of the last few to leave. She could hear it in their voices as they phoned to their parents to say they were coming home. That the heroes they hoped to become were nobodies. That their parents should expect them back.

And then, she imagined, they would tell their families to expect the worst. That even prayer won't work. They knew now what they were too naïve to know only weeks ago — this world, as they knew it, was ending.

Thea hated it.

She hadn't been fighting forces of evil as long as Oscar, sure; but she still had the right to disagree with him. If it was up to her, she would arm these recruits for battle and fight to the last. If they were to go down with the world anyway, what would it matter if they all went out fighting?

It would be far better than the whimper with which they were going out now.

She wondered what Julian might say, should he still be with them.

Julian never hid his emotions, nor did he ever try to appease someone with comforting words. He said things as he saw them, and everyone always knew how he felt.

Yet, Thea really wasn't sure how he would feel about this.

Would he agree with Oscar and give up?

She shook her head. That didn't sound like the Julian she knew. The Julian she knew would go down with his army.

But what could Thea do?

She was powerful, yes. A Sensitive was a person conceived by Heaven, which gave them abilities to fight demons and explore the paranormal. They had discovered that some Sensitives have more of Heaven in them — she was the one with the most. She could command demons in a way others couldn't.

But that still wasn't enough. The hope she had originally given Oscar, April and Julian had faded when they realised that, however strong Thea's gift was, it was still not strong enough.

A teenage girl, probably fifteen, pulled a large suitcase through the doorway. A taxi waited for her, the driver doing nothing to help. Thea rushed over, took one side of the trunk, and helped the girl to lift it into the car boot.

"Thanks," said the girl, timidly, her eyes avoiding Thea's.

"You're welcome," Thea answered then, without meaning to, added, "I'm sorry."

The girl looked at her, confused. "For what?"

It was a good question.

What exactly was Thea sorry for?

She looked around, at the building, at the empty windows and quiet rooms.

"This," Thea answered. "You could have been so much more."

"I'm not going to stop."

"Excuse me?"

"I mean, I say it with full respect. I respect you, and I respect Oscar, and I respect April — but you've taught me lessons that can't be untaught. I can't go back now."

Thea marvelled at this young girl and her shy resolve. She seemed shy, yet spoke with so much conviction that Thea could tell that she meant it.

"You can't just teach us these abilities then expect us to go to sleep at night without worrying about what's under our bed. I know too much now. I know you all think we're doomed, but that means we have nothing to lose, right? I might be going home, but I'm sure there will still be plenty of demons for me to fight there."

Thea took a moment to study this girl. Too thin, dyed hair, lots of bracelets. She reminded Thea of April, and she imagined the two of them would have been good friends.

Under different circumstances, that is.

"Good for you," Thea responded.

She held out her hand, and the girl shook it.

"Good luck," Thea added.

"Same to you," the girl said as she stepped into the back of the taxi. Thea watched as the taxi took off and disappeared around the corner.

It gave her a sense of satisfaction that at least one student had learnt something. That they wouldn't go back on all the lessons they'd been taught, just because they were being told to go home.

Thea turned to go, but was stopped by a familiar face.

"Henry," she said. "Why haven't you left yet?"

Henry was a remarkable young man. Only a few years younger than her, he had arrived for training with no confidence. He had since helped Thea tremendously whilst fighting off the possessed a few days ago, just as Oscar and April had attempted to confront The Devil in Hell.

For a moment, she wondered what would have happened if Oscar and April hadn't tried something so foolish and doomed to failure.

"I'm not going," said Henry.

"What do you mean, everyone is–"

"I know. But you still need help."

"Henry, I–"

"I know you do. April is possessed. You're going to need help."

"Henry, look–"

"Even if it's just fetching you coffee, or water to keep you going, whatever, I don't care. You showed me something and I don't plan to forget it."

"We all need coffee and water, I guess.".

Thea smiled. Henry had changed so much in the past few weeks. After battling by each other's side, Thea considered him a friend. With Oscar so occupied with April, she only had the one. It would do no harm to have him there with her while Oscar was preoccupied with his misery.

"Let's go home," Thea said.

She looked back at the empty building one more time, then they left, never to return.

4

THE AIR GREW COLDER AS OSCAR CLIMBED THE STAIRS. THE route to what used to be the bedroom he shared with the love of his life was now an ominous, dreaded walk.

He had quoted Psalm 23:4 at demons he was exorcising before: *Even though I walk through the valley of the shadow of death...*

Yet, only now, did he understand what those words meant. Only now did he feel he was actually walking such a walk.

The door at the end of the corridor was ajar. A narrow crack let only a little light out, for there was little light in there to begin with. He could hear breathing; heavy, croaky, wicked breathing.

Oscar put his arms around himself, shivering. The hairs on his arms stood on end. He stepped slowly, not wanting to enter the room, but knowing he must.

Inside that room was April's body, but he had no idea if April was still there. If only she hadn't gone after Oscar. If only he hadn't left in the first place. If only The Devil hadn't tempted them to Hell so he could come back in the body of a conduit.

If only, if only, if only.

Two stupid words he was tired of repeating.

It meant nothing. But then again, everything was for nothing now, wasn't it?

He placed his fingers against the door. Nudged it open. Allowed it to creak just wide enough that he could fit in.

He did not enter yet. He stood, watching the body on the bed, wrists bound to the headboard and ankles bound to the end of the bed.

He turned away. He'd seen this image every day, but it was getting worse. She was getting paler. Weaker. Scratches from the inside were coming through her skin.

Were those scratches from April? Was it her soul trying to get out? Or was it just another torment for Oscar to suffer?

Honestly, he didn't know how much longer the restraints would last. A creature like The Devil, the king of Hell, an entity made of the purest evil, would not be held back for long. Oscar knew his opponent was just gathering his strength, that he was just getting used to this body and this world. Soon enough, The Devil would break out, and Oscar would walk upstairs to find April gone.

But what was he supposed to do? The rites of exorcism were doing nothing. He had no power over it. Not even Thea, with her stronger powers, had managed to make any progress.

"Are you going to stand there all day?" it asked. Its voice was deep. Cocky. Arrogant.

Oscar waited a moment, stepped inside, walked around the bed and watched, as the thing destroying his girlfriend watched him back.

"So what is it today?" it continued. "Which prayers are you going to try?"

He stood at the end of the bed. Arms crossed. Trying to look like he was in charge, even though they both knew he wasn't.

"I need you to let her eat," he said.

It raised her eyebrows.

"You need her body. You won't be able to use it if she starves to death."

"I don't need it for long."

"But you still need it for now. And a human body requires food. And water."

It laughed.

"Laugh all you want, but–"

April's crotch rose into the air and a large, elongated scream pushed out of her cracked lips. It was a piercing screech, so full of agony; a mixture of The Devil's roar and April's pain.

Oscar flinched away. He could hear April's voice among the shrieks.

He knew he shouldn't let it affect him. It was integral to an exorcism that you do not let the demon get to you. It was crucial.

But everything he'd learned was void now. Everything he knew didn't matter. He had no way of getting this thing out of April's body. Nothing worked. He had lost, and he was just trying to keep the body alive for...

For what?

Some kind of absent hope he had buried deep down?

Some kind of belief that he may get her back some day?

No, of course not. It was purely for selfish reasons.

He was keeping her alive because he couldn't bear to lose that last piece of April that remained — her body.

A good man would just let her die and banish The Devil in doing so.

But he was not a good man anymore. He was a defeated man, and he cared little for doing the right thing.

Derek and Julian were gone. They were the wise ones. Not him.

Finally, the scream ended, and the body fell back to the bed.

"What's the matter?" it said, spreading her legs. "You miss her?"

Her crotch was exposed. It was bloody.

Once, he'd looked at her naked body and been taken by its beauty. Now he was stumped by its quick and severe degradation.

"As soon as I get free of these ropes…"

Oscar tried not to be bated.

"I am going to fuck your kitchen knife, fuck barbed wire, fuck every man who–"

"Stop it!"

Oscar turned away.

It laughed. Hard. At him.

He didn't even bother to be brave. What was the point?

He looked back at it. His eyes hurt from lack of sleep.

It would have been better if Oscar had chosen the world instead of April. At least, if she had died then, he would have saved her from this fate.

He walked out of the room. He closed the door, but it did nothing. He could still hear the laughter and the screams throughout the house. It was constant. It felt like someone digging their fingers into his head and screaming as his brain expanded and…

He covered his ears and sat on the bottom step.

He could still hear it.

What he'd give to just be able to fall asleep.

5

OSCAR ALLOWED HIMSELF A WALK. A SMALL LUXURY. SUCH A seemingly insignificant thing — but something that made such a difference.

Thea wasn't back yet. He had no idea where she was, or what she was wasting her time doing. He'd left a radio in the corner of April's room, and he had a single headphone running up the inside of his hoodie and into his ear. That way, he could always know what was happening — but it also meant he could never escape the prison of that room. No matter how clear the skies, how delightful the day, how big the smile of a passing stranger, The Devil's deep, croaky breathing was always there in his ear.

He passed a coffee shop. He considered going in, and even placed his hand on the door, but a memory stopped him.

All those years ago, when he was just a timid boy in his late teens, trying to confess his adoration for April, this was the coffee shop he would take her to. He'd psych himself up, decide on the words, but when he sat and looked at her nothing would come out. On reflection, she was always hopeful — she'd see the words edging to his lips, waiting for him to tell her how he felt, just to see him give up.

Shortly after, he had to save Derek from a prison occupied by a powerful entity. That was tough — yet it was preferable to trying to muster the confidence to admit his feelings.

He could see the table through the window where they had sat. Another couple sat there, the man's hand resting on the woman's. His thumb stroked her fingers, and they smiled. They didn't say much. They probably didn't need to. They were too besotted for idle chatter.

Oscar hated them.

He felt his lip lifting into a sneer. His head was shaking, and he was imagining striding in there and destroying the joyful moment.

"You're going to die, you know!" he could say. "No matter how much you love each other, it doesn't mean shit. You will be torn apart and tortured and you will not choose to save each other — you will only think of yourself."

Oh, the pleasure it would bring him to tell them how short-lived their happiness would be, and how pointless it was. He hated them. Despised them. *Loathed* them.

He wanted to hurt them.

A low-pitched chuckle came through his headphones. It was as if The Devil knew what Oscar was thinking; as if it could sense the anger Oscar was feeling.

Oscar turned away from the coffee shop. He passed a lone polystyrene cup some prick had littered on the floor, now being pushed around by the wind. He swung his foot through it. It flew across the street, landing in the road, only to dance around the floor again.

Someone walking past looked at him. A child. Staring in that infuriating way children often do; as if their age gives them the liberty to be rude.

"What?" Oscar grunted.

The child turned their face away and walked on, taking hold of their mother's hand.

Across the street, a busker sang about the conquering ability of love. A few people stood around him, gathered like disciples, listening to the lessons this singer was singing.

This man and his messages of love... what did he know? Had he ever sacrificed the world for the woman he loved?

No, he most likely hadn't. So, whatever song he was ruining, it was insincere.

Oscar hated him. And he hated those gathered around him, encouraging him. The man tapping his foot, the woman nodding her head, the couple putting their arms around each other like the lyrics actually meant something to them — they could all fuck off.

They knew nothing of the world. They knew nothing of what was rising up, and they knew nothing of the genuine sacrifices that come with love.

He hated them. Each and every one of them.

He hated them so, so much.

Yet, at the same time, he envied their ignorance. He wished he could be so unaware, so oblivious to what was happening.

He wished he could tap his foot, nod his head, or tuck his arm around April. He wished he could listen to this man's words and pretend they meant something. He wished...

Wishing did nothing.

No one cared what he wished for.

No one ever had.

The laughter in his ear died down, and the croaky breathing resumed.

He'd left the house for too long. He shouldn't have left at all. It was time he returned.

He glanced back at the busker, at the coffee shop, and at the couple inside.

Instead of a sneer, his face twisted into tears — but he kept them inside.

He'd rather learn to feel nothing than to feel all this.

He walked back home, hands in his pockets, head down, avoiding eye contact with everyone he passed.

6

Thea felt the same ominous feeling she felt every time she approached the house she now called home. When she'd first moved in, April was eager to teach her, Oscar was driven, and Julian was bringing through fresh recruits.

Now the house, seemingly cast in a permanent shadow, did not give her the sense of enthusiasm it previously had. Now, all it gave her was despondency.

She did not want to have to face Oscar in his current state, and she definitely did not want to face April in hers.

Nevertheless, with Henry at her side, she unlocked the door and gave it a gentle push.

No lights were on. Oscar sat on the bottom step, his head leant against the wall, his eyes closed, used to the raucous noise coming from above.

A clatter shook the ceiling.

Oscar's eyes opened, and his body remained still. Those eyes glanced at Thea, then to Henry.

"What's he doing here?" he asked.

"Henry has come to help."

"Help what?"

"The fight."

"There is no fight."

"Not for you, but–"

"Give it up, Thea. You're young. I know, I was once. The fight is over."

He marched into the kitchen.

"Maybe I should go," Henry suggested quietly.

"You are not going," she said. "Just — wait in there while I talk to him."

She gestured to the living room. Henry obediently shuffled in, and Thea closed the door behind him. She hesitated, then walked into the kitchen to find Oscar leaning at the sink, drinking straight from the tap.

"Don't you use a glass anymore?" she asked.

"What are you now, my mum?" Oscar said. He ran the water over his hands, then over his face. He straightened his back, closing his eyes and stretching his neck.

"I really think–"

"You still haven't answered my question."

Thea looked bemused. "What question?"

"What is he doing here?"

Oscar gestured at the door that led to the living room.

Thea stood defiantly.

"I asked him to come," she said.

"Why? What's the point? What is he going to do?"

"If the world's going to end, I'd like a friend here."

Oscar snorted. "He's a friend now?"

"We fought side by side. Often, that makes people close. I thought you might know about that."

Oscar dropped his head. Closed his eyes.

Thea was certain Oscar knew what a dick he was being, but she felt sorry for him. He'd caused this, yes — but he'd also put every bit of blood and sweat in his body into fighting it. He'd felt hope that things would get better many times, only to have that hope pulled away from him over and over. He'd been through so much to get to this point, he had risked everything, and all he had to show for it was the abhorrent state the love of his life was in.

"I'm sorry, Oscar," Thea said.

"Sorry for what?"

"I'm just... sorry. I know this is hard for you."

Oscar shook his head. He muttered something that she couldn't hear.

"Let me ask you something." She folded her arms and looked inquisitively at him, ignoring the sceptical look on his face. "What if you exorcised April?"

Oscar turned and huffed, throwing his arms into the air as if to say *this again?*

"Hear me out," Thea said. "Please."

"I've heard you out already."

"Then hear me out again."

"It's no use."

"Just one more time. Please."

"Don't you see? All this does is prolong the pain, increase the torture — it's done. The more you don't accept that, the more it hurts."

"Fine. The last time. Just humour me."

Oscar shook his head, took a deep breath.

"What?" he finally said.

"Say you manage to exorcise the thing in April, right, and–"

"The thing in April is The Devil, Thea. It's not a demon, it's not even a prince of Hell, it is the ruler; it is the epitome of everything that is evil. It's too strong to beat. Even for you. It's not possible."

"You said you'd humour me."

"Fine. What then?"

"Say you manage to exorcise it, you would defeat The Devil, right?"

"Which is–"

"Impossible, I know. But say you did."

Oscar shrugged. "Then you would defeat The Devil."

"Okay, and if you did that…"

She considered her next words, knowing she already had a tough audience, wanting to be precise and persuasive in what she was about to say.

"Right," she tried, "remember when this all happened, yeah? You and the Sensitives went into some other place that meant you weren't here on Earth to keep the balance of Heaven and Hell. The balanced shifted toward Hell, which allowed all this to happen. That correct?"

"Yes."

"Right, well — say you removed The Devil from April's body, and removed him from this world. A current balance between Hell and Heaven has been established, has become the new *normal* — so if you disrupt that…"

"Then what?"

"Surely that would push the balance in Heaven's favour."

"In theory."

"Well, an angel is the opposite of a demon, right?"

"Again, in theory."

"Surely the balance shifting against Hell would mean an increase in angelic activity, meaning that Heaven will temporarily have a stronger ability to remove demons, then we–"

"Thea, Thea, please, just stop."

She stopped. Watched him run his hands through his hair. He opened a drawer to look for paracetamol. There was none.

"If you defeat The Devil," she said, "you would defeat Hell. It would give us hope, right?"

Oscar grimaced and sighed again.

"Right," he said. "Again, in theory, yes. Defeating him would shift the balance back into our favour and allow Heaven to intervene and reduce demonic activity. The original balance could then be restored."

"So that's what we have to do, then!"

Oscar raised his clenched fist and gesticulated at her.

"You're not getting it!"

"No, Oscar, I–"

He picked up a glass from the drying board and threw it across the room, smashing it into hundreds of pieces. He strode forward, grabbed Thea's arms, and glared into her eyes.

"It cannot be done. We cannot beat The Devil."

There was a knock at the front door.

Oscar didn't move. Neither did Thea.

The knock came again.

Thea shoved Oscar's hands off of her and called out, "Henry, please get that."

"Why?" Oscar said.

"Huh?"

"Why answer the door? Who could possibly matter enough to answer the door to?"

The sound of the front door opening and closing filled the uncomfortable silence. Seconds later, Henry walked in.

"Guys, there's someone here to see you," he said.

"We don't care," Oscar answered.

"He says he's from the Church."

Oscar and Thea exchanged a look.

"He said his name is Father Lorenzo Romano."

7

Oscar had instructed Henry to go watch April while they spoke with the man from the Church.

Henry did not want to do this but, already feeling useless and unwelcome, he did not want to make himself appear to have no purpose for being there.

He just really did not want to be in a room with it.

He approached the door, hearing the shuddering breaths, feeling the ominous evil.

That was one thing he'd noticed about being a Sensitive — the feelings. He was more in tune with them now, more able to know what they were. They weren't just random pangs of emotion; they were his gift, trying to guide him and teach him.

He stepped inside. The woman — although she did not look much like a woman anymore — was bound to the bed.

The thing inside of her went still and silent. Its head, and only its head, turned toward him with a lecherous smile.

Henry edged toward a wooden chair and sat down, keeping his eyes on it the entire time; just as it kept its eyes on him.

It smiled widely. An open-mouthed smile, as if it was waiting for the big punchline.

Henry shivered. This room was far colder than any other.

"They must be desperate," it finally said.

Henry went to reply, then remembered what Oscar and Thea had taught him: a demon will try to bate you. A demon will do all it can to tempt you into conversation, to engage with you, so it can grow its hold over you. The last thing he wanted to do was give it any more strength than it had.

"To send in a boy like this. What are you, twelve? Thirteen?"

"I am sixteen."

He flinched. Cursed himself. That was too easy. What was wrong with him?

"Aw, what's the matter? Did I get you already?"

It had.

Why was Henry even here?

Why did it need looking after?

He wondered whether this was a test. Oscar wanted to test his resolve, test whether he was worthy of being in this house. If you couldn't handle sitting in a room with it, how were you supposed to handle fighting it?

"Have you told your parents yet?"

Told my parents what?

He wanted to say it, and he went to say it, but stopped himself.

"They must be so disappointed... Disapproving, religious parents... The only thing you ever did to make them proud was be a Sensitive... How will they feel now they know you've lost?"

How did it know all this?

It must hear Oscar and Thea talk. It's stuck in a house with them, it must hear everything.

304

"I'd be disappointed by a timid little child like you too."

"Is this the best you got?" he said, attempting to show some resilience.

It smiled again, wider, unnaturally so.

It spoke again, but this time, it was not in its own voice.

It was in Henry's mother's voice.

"Oh, Henry. What have you done? How have you managed to let us down all over again?"

How was it doing this? How was it mimicking her voice? How did it know these things?

"Henry, I hope you know, there is no place for you at home."

He shook his head. This wasn't his mother. It was just a poor imitation.

"I want to fuck you, Henry."

What?

"I want you inside of me, Henry."

It wasn't a poor imitation. It wasn't even an imitation. It *was* his mother's voice. Exactly. Every inflexion and every rising and lowering of pitch was just as she would speak.

And she was saying these things to him.

"I want to put your cock in me like I do with your father's. Oh, please, Henry, please do it, please put your cock in me."

It spread April's legs.

Beneath the blood stains, her cunt invited him.

"You know you want to…"

Henry stood.

He couldn't stand it anymore.

"Touch it."

He turned to the wall. Folded his arms. He wouldn't let it win.

"Rape me, Henry. Rape me like your father does."

Henry turned around and, with a large roar that broke his voice, he shouted: "*No!*"

It laughed.

"Got you," it said.

8

Father Lorenzo Romano sat on the edge of the sofa, the cup of tea he had been reluctantly offered in his hand.

Thea sat on the other side of the sofa, on its edge.

Oscar leant against the windowsill on the other side of the room.

Lorenzo slowly brought the cup to his mouth, took a sip, then lowered it once more. He did not look at the others.

"I'm sure you haven't travelled all the way from Rome to drink our tea. How about you get on with whatever you're here for?"

Lorenzo hesitated. Stared at the cup.

"Or is it just another visit to remind me how much I fucked up?"

"That's not what we–"

"That's all you do. Blame me, cover stuff up, then blame me some more. I bet you all have meetings in the Vatican where you slag me off just for the sake of slagging me off."

"You did do this."

"I know!" He stood. "Now fuck off."

Oscar went to leave the room, but halted as Lorenzo spoke.

"Wait. Please."

He turned to Lorenzo expectantly.

"We have a possible solution... I think it would be worth hearing this."

Oscar returned to the windowsill, leaning against it and folding his arms.

"Go on," he prompted.

Lorenzo took another sip of tea, then spoke.

"There is a man in Korea who, it is said, defeated The Devil."

"He defeated The Devil?"

"So it is said."

"And you only thought to tell me this now?"

"He is not... I mean, he does not follow... I..."

"Lorenzo, I am losing patience."

"He is not Catholic." He blurted it out like he was ripping off a plaster. "Nor is he any denomination of Christianity."

"What is he then? Muslim? Hindu?"

"He is a Buddhist."

"Ah, I see."

For people who taught their congregations to be accepting of others, Oscar had imagined they would be more open to hearing how people from various backgrounds had defeated evil — but apparently not.

"So how did he defeat The Devil?" Oscar asked.

"Well, he says he defeated Mara. That is their version of The Devil — or, at least, that's what they call their equivalent."

"So how did he do it?"

"We don't know. We have never spoken to him."

Oscar stared at Lorenzo, dumbfounded. He couldn't

believe they had a resource like this and had allowed a difference of religion to stop them from using it.

"I thought your religion preached tolerance," Oscar said. "I thought you all worked in harmony, all linking and coinciding, all–"

"Yes, yes, I get your point."

Lorenzo shifted uncomfortably. He grimaced, and his face contorted as if he was chewing something really disgusting.

"I suppose you are right," Lorenzo said. "We preach tolerance, and we should show it. We will work with this man for the sake of this war."

"That's big of you."

"Lorenzo," interjected Thea, "if we defeat The Devil, would that be it? I mean, would we win?"

Lorenzo paused to think.

"Mostly, yes. There would still be more demonic activity than we would like, but, ultimately, it would shift the balance long enough for Heaven to do its work."

Oscar shook his head.

"Funny," he said. "When you showed up, I thought you were here to put a knife across April's throat, hoping it would defeat The Devil."

"It would not. Believe me, we have entertained the idea, and should it be the solution, we would not have hesitated."

Lorenzo and Oscar locked eyes for a moment; determination versus aggression.

"Guys," Thea said. "That's not the case, so let's drop it, yeah?"

Lorenzo stood.

"I think I am done here."

Lorenzo took out an envelope and passed it to Oscar. Oscar stared at it, then took it.

"These are plane tickets," Lorenzo said. "They will get you

to Korea. The plane leaves tonight. His name is Om Samsara. Good luck."

Lorenzo walked out of the room, followed a few seconds later by the sound of the front door opening and shutting.

Oscar and Thea looked at each other.

"That's hope, right?" she said. "I mean, it's a chance?"

Oscar opened the envelope. Sure enough, the ticket's time stamp was scheduled for tonight.

He stuffed them in his back pocket and walked upstairs.

9

OSCAR STOOD AT THE END OF THE BED, LOOKING OVER APRIL'S body. He tried to see her as April, but he couldn't; not anymore.

There was nothing of that sweet face, that naughty smile, that caring look…

It had been decimated. Ruined. Distorted, torn and destroyed.

This thing was all he saw now.

He wondered if she could ever return. If the scars could be undone. If the way that The Devil had stolen her body and wounded it, stretched it, and corrupted it, could ever be undone. He wondered if April would be the same should she return.

He struggled to see the face he once kissed, and the fingers that would touch him so softly and make his entire body tingle.

Still, he tried.

"I am speaking to April," he said.

"April's not here right now."

It was so cocky, so self-assured. Grinning at him. Showing off that it was in full control.

He ignored it.

"April, I don't know if you can hear me, and I don't know if you are in there, but…"

"April is busy getting fucked in Hell."

He shook his head. Forced the words to become nothing but white noise.

If April was in there, she would hear him. He had to ignore The Devil's interjections. He had to pretend they weren't there.

"But I'm on it. I have a plan. I have… Something."

"You… have… nothing…"

"April, if you are in there, I want you to know, I'm not giving up. Not yet. I have something I'm trying, and I don't know if it will work, but I have to go away for a while, just…"

He struggled to speak. Struggled to say the three words he wanted to say, knowing they would be mocked and ridiculed.

He said them anyway.

"I love you."

It laughed.

Oh, how it laughed.

If it was not bound to the bed, it would have rolled off. Tears streamed down her face; guffaws filled the room. It was difficult to know if it was genuine hilarity at the thought that Oscar could win, or whether it was forced laughter, designed to taunt him.

He turned to leave.

"How sweet," it said as the laughter died down. "We love you too. Both of us."

Oscar paused by the door. Looked over his shoulder.

"I'll pass the message on once we've finished with her," it said.

He strode slowly forward, approaching the bed, shaking his head, feeling a sense of defiance overcome him.

"Now I am speaking to The Devil," he said. "Or, at least, the shit stain who tries to taint April's body."

"After all this time, how can you talk to me like that…"

"Know this — you have not won."

It laughed again.

It always bloody laughed.

Oscar looked forward to when it stopped laughing. When he could rip that laughter out of her body. When it screamed instead.

"To you who have tried to tear us apart," Oscar continued, "who have tried to make us feel bad, make us feel like we had no hope, like you had won — you have not."

"Beg to differ…"

"You haven't. Not yet."

Although he didn't feel it, although he was forcing the confidence, he enjoyed his moment of fightback. He enjoyed telling that thing that, with some modicum of sincerity, there was an opportunity, however wayward and hopeless it was.

Did Oscar really believe some Buddhist in Korea would have the answers?

Honestly, no.

Did The Devil look scared?

Not at all. If anything, it looked even more enthralled by the idea of Oscar fighting, turned on by the anticipation of more conflict.

But at least, for now, Oscar could entertain the idea that someone may have the answers.

That April would not be lost forever.

That this world could be salvaged; however little he considered it worth salvaging.

The odds were against him.

But, then again, they always had been.

THEA AND HENRY STOOD IN THE HALLWAY, WATCHING helplessly as Oscar readied himself, ignoring all the commotion from above them.

Thea wasn't sure whether Oscar was ignoring the noise because he was used to it, or because he had no choice. Either way, he persisted, and he was standing at the front door with a bag of clothes within an hour.

He looked back at Thea and Henry. He didn't appear as angry as he had been for the past few days — instead, he looked sad. Broken. With bags under his eyes and a lack of colour in his cheeks. Thea could see in his face just how much April's torment was destroying him.

"You look like two scared kids," he said.

Thea laughed. It wasn't said in a mocking or scornful way, but as an observation that Thea and Henry fully agreed with.

The laughter was small and short-lived, however, and the empty silence quickly returned.

An enormous bang came from upstairs. Oscar looked upwards for a moment, then back to Thea.

"I'm relying on you to take care of her." He looked to Henry, too. "Both of you."

Thea nodded.

"It will get stronger," Oscar added. "The restraints are keeping it tied down for now, but... I don't know how long that will last. Days, if that. And I don't know how long this will take. Hopefully quickly, but..."

He looked away. Bit his bottom lip.

Thea could see the tears he was not willing to let out.

Maybe she hadn't realised just how much this battle had worn away at him. He had barely left the house as he was reluctant to leave April alone — yet there was no room where you could not hear it. It was constant. Whatever he did and wherever he went, he had to listen to the torture of the woman he loved.

"We'll look after her," Thea said, trying to sound calm and in control, trying to provide as much reassurance as she could. She had a feeling no amount of reassurance would be good enough.

"It will help keep it a little under control if you read the exorcism rites," Oscar suggested. "I mean, it won't do anything, really, but it can't hurt. Just a little a day. Hopefully, it will delay it growing stronger."

"I thought it took about a year for amalgamation incarnation to occur," Henry said, looking between them.

"That's with a normal demon," Oscar replied. "This is not a normal demon. And April is not a normal host — she is a conduit. She is more susceptible. We can't know how long. It could be as little as weeks until it's fully–"

Oscar stopped.

He couldn't say it. He just couldn't say it.

Thea stepped forward. Put her arms around him.

She felt him cry into her shoulder but, when she stepped

back, she saw no tears; he was determined not to show any weakness.

"I just hope this isn't all for nothing," Oscar said. "If we lose her completely, or if she dies, and I'm not here–"

"Then I will make sure that, before she goes, she knows that you are still fighting for her."

He nodded.

He looked at Henry and nodded again.

He went to speak, but didn't.

He picked up his bag. Turned. Opened the front door. Stepped out.

Looked over his shoulder.

"I trust you," he said. "Don't let me down."

"We won't."

Oscar left. Thea shut the door, stepped back into the hallway, and resumed her place by Henry's side.

The ceiling shook again.

Thea and Henry found their hands entwining. Not out of any feeling of attraction or love, but of fear, and a need to share this fear.

After all, they were alone with The Devil now.

There was no one else coming to help them.

11

THE DRIVE TO LONDON HAD TAKEN THREE HOURS.

The flight would take eleven hours.

Then God knows how long it would take to find this place once Oscar arrived. If he even did.

He hadn't been to Korea and did not know what to expect. He did not know how to get a bus or a taxi, and he did not trust himself driving down a busy street on the opposite side of the road. Yet he had to get to a temple, in the middle of nowhere, that had not been used for many, many years.

Lorenzo could have given more help than just booking a plane ticket and assuming Oscar was going to leap onboard with no objection.

But that's what Lorenzo does, isn't it? Expect the Sensitives to wage the Church's war and hate them for any destruction that may occur as a result.

His leg bounced. He huffed. He felt impatient.

What was he even doing?

Going to see some Buddhist in a temple...

What was he expecting to learn that he didn't know already?

He'd been fighting demons for years. He'd faced all kinds, and he'd confronted The Devil in Hell. What could someone who had isolated themselves from the world know about the war he was waging?

The air stewardess paused by Oscar. Asked if he'd like a coffee. Oscar asked if they had a beer. They did.

He ordered two.

He poured the first into the plastic cup provided, drank half down in one, then rested his head back and closed his eyes.

He was not restful, but he had to try. He had a lengthy flight ahead of him. He hadn't thought to pick up a book to occupy his mind — such thoughts seemed ridiculous at the time.

All he could think about was leaving April at home.

Well, whatever was in April's body was at home... Oscar had no idea where April was.

What happens to a soul when it is pushed out of its body?

Hell, supposedly.

Funny, really. He'd fought to save souls, but he'd never really questioned what he was saving them from.

He wished Derek was still there to provide the answers. Or, as much as he hated admitting it, he'd gladly make do with Julian. Despite his impatient demeanour and constant condescension toward Oscar, he had been a good friend. Oscar was only just starting to see that now.

Julian would always be Julian. He would be who he was; an irritable, stubborn individual who flung disparaging remarks around like a child's entertainer might fling sweets to their audience.

But that was who he was. There was no real malice in it.

And, more than anything, Julian cared deeply for April.

He had taken her off the streets and taught her how to use her gift. Even though Oscar hadn't been on the streets, Julian had done a similar thing with him — he had taken him from a dull, monotonous life that was going nowhere and given him a purpose.

Oscar bet that, wherever Julian was now, he regretted bringing Oscar into the battle. If he hadn't, maybe he would still be alive and the world would be saved.

Oscar raised his cup, tilting it to the memory of his lost friend, and drank the rest of its contents.

He looked around.

Everyone was so clueless. No one knew. All the horrors that had been occurring in the world, the increased amount of violence, and none of these people really knew why.

A woman was sitting across from him, her child next to her, giving him crayons and helping him look through his colouring book. She was a mother doing anything she can to keep her child occupied for a lengthy journey. Her biggest concern was whether her child would get restless. She had no idea what she should really be worried about.

An elderly couple sat a few rows back. Holding hands. Probably in their eighties, yet still holding hands. As if it was still just as special as it was when they were young. If this plane went down, they would go down together. They had no regrets.

A man in a suit sat on the seat across the aisle. Laptop open, tapping away, getting work done.

He resented each of them for their ignorance, yet envied their unawareness.

They would all probably be dead within the coming months.

Dead or tortured. Whichever fate befell them.

Unless this man, this… what was his name? What had Lorenzo said?

Ah, yes. Om Samsara.

Unless this Om Samsara had some answers as to how they could defeat The Devil — or Mara, as Om apparently called it.

Who was Oscar kidding? What the hell would this man know?

This was stupid, and he wanted to go back. He wanted to be with April before he lost her completely, just so she would know, however deep she was buried, that he was still there, still by her side.

Everything infuriated him. Lorenzo's resolve to keep going, this long flight, The Devil, Thea's naivety, the world for not knowing — and he didn't stop there. He thought back to his childhood, resenting his parents for having too high expectations, and hating the boy who bullied him at school.

Ten hours of the flight left.

He closed his eyes and tried to get some sleep, however unlikely that would be.

THEN

FOUR YEARS OLD

1 2

THE CLASSROOM FELT CROWDED. IT ALWAYS DID. IT WASN'T, but it felt that way.

Oscar was so much smaller than the other children.

Not that much smaller, but again, that was how it felt.

He sat on the second row in from the back, next to the window, and found himself spending most of the day staring out of it. He could see the playground and, beyond that, bushes, and beyond that, a house with a swing set and an older lady who was always gardening.He wondered why, with an older lady living there, she had a swing set. He speculated that maybe she had a granddaughter — only Oscar had never seen a granddaughter there.

"Oscar?"

Oscar quickly turned his head. His teacher, Mrs McNeil, was looking at him expectantly, as were the rest of the class.

All the other children, all twenty-something of them; staring at him.

He'd been asked a question, he knew it. Only he hadn't been paying attention. He didn't know what the question was.

He looked around for help.

"What do you think, Oscar?" repeated Mrs McNeil.

Oscar did not know what he thought, as he did not know what he was being asked about.

He tried to remember what this lesson was. Was it maths? English? Something else?

Letters were written on the board. *A B C D E F G H I.*

"Come on," urged Mrs McNeil.

Why was everyone staring at him so much? They were all smiling, like they knew something he didn't, like they enjoyed how scared he looked.

"I — I don't know," he said.

"Sure you do. Just come up with an idea."

In front of him, a boy turned around. His name was Bertrand.

Oscar did not like Bertrand.

Bertrand was mean.

He was pudgy and had meaty hands. He had these spots on his cheek, and his hair was always messy. Yet, despite these flaws, no one ever dared be nasty to him. He was always the nasty one. Kids would always do what he told them, even if it meant hurting someone else, so long as it meant they didn't get hurt instead.

"Just one word, that's all I'm after."

One word about what?

Bertrand's smile widened. He was taking pleasure out of this.

Oscar was too young to know when someone was being vindictive, but he was old enough to feel ashamed. He couldn't explain the feeling, but he felt it. Bertrand was making him feel terrible, and he didn't like it, and he wished that everyone would stop looking at him.

"Just one word beginning with I, that's all I need."

A word beginning with I?

Is that what she wanted?

Oscar tried to think.

A word beginning with I, then he'd be left alone…

"Igloo," Oscar suggested.

"Not quite," Mrs McNeil said. "Bertrand already said that one. Try thinking of one of your own."

"Yeah, dick face," whispered Bertrand, so quiet only he and Oscar could hear him. "Think of another one."

Everyone was still staring.

Everyone.

Staring.

He didn't like it.

He didn't.

His heart raced.

He breathed quicker and quicker.

Tears accumulated in the corner of his eyes.

"Come on, Oscar," urged Mrs McNeil.

"Yeah, come on, Oscar," spat Bertrand.

Oscar couldn't take it anymore.

He couldn't.

He couldn't take it.

He stood. His chair fell over. His desk shoved forward. He ran from the classroom, into the corridor outside, and sat on the bench beneath the coat pegs.

He buried his face in his hands and cried.

Class ended five minutes later.

The other kids came out of the classroom to put their coats on, table by table, until the classroom was empty but for the teacher.

"Why don't you come in?" she said to Oscar. "Let's have a chat."

She walked back inside the classroom, expecting Oscar to follow.

Oscar stood.

Bertrand was next to him. He hadn't seen him arrive, nor had he heard him approach. He was just there. Grinning.

"You're a fucking loser," he said.

Oscar didn't know what that meant.

"I will kill you someday."

Bertrand walked away, coat in hand, into the playground.

Oscar returned to the classroom, not hearing a word his teacher said.

NOW

13

THE TAXI DROVE FOR AN HOUR AND COST AN EXTORTIONATE amount of money. He wasn't particularly bothered about going into his overdraft, considering the world was about to end — but, after an eleven-hour flight in a seat where his legs wouldn't fit behind the chair in front, he was already in a bad enough mood.

The driver let Oscar out at the base of a hill, and left before Oscar could ask where he was meant to go. As it was, after a walk of twenty minutes or so up a path that took him around the circumference of the hill and through a steep forest, he came to some stone steps.

He decided this must be it. He was finally there. Hurrah, journey over!

Except, as his eyes rose up the stairs, he realised he couldn't see their end.

"Of course," he muttered.

His legs were cramped from the travelling and already aching from walking uphill. The last thing he wanted to do was climb a mass of stairs.

What if the temple wasn't even at the top of these stairs, and they just led to nothing?

But then again, what else was he supposed to go? Google Maps wasn't much help, and he could hardly just phone up the reclusive Buddhist that lived here for directions. The steps seemed like the only choice and, if he wanted a bed to sleep on that night that wasn't made of twigs and insects, he would have to climb the steps.

With a huff, he began.

Up the first, up the second. Ten steps and he already had to pause.

Why were these people always a recluse? He couldn't remember the last time he went for help from someone who wasn't shut away in their house or in some obscure part of the world.

He continued onwards. He tried taking two steps at a time to see if that would help, but it didn't seem to make him climb any quicker.

He looked back and could no longer see the beginning.

He looked up and still could not see the top.

This better be worth it.

He continued.

As he rose higher, he tried using his hands, pulling his body upwards, helping to ease the pressure on his legs.

The top finally came into sight.

"Oh, thank you..."

He forced the final bit of energy to his legs and pushed himself up, and up, and up, until he reached the top step and threw himself to the floor.

He lay, looking up at the darkening sky. Panting.

No one came to see him. No one greeted. This Buddhist bloke was obviously somewhere asleep or watching from afar and laughing at him.

Oscar waited for some energy to return to his body.

It didn't.

His back hurt from the bumps of the stone, so he sat up. Looked around.

Stone rooms surrounded him. No doors, just blackness. It didn't look like this place was connected to electricity. But then again, why would it? May as well keep everything as medieval as possible!

He pushed himself to his feet. Stepped forward. His light steps echoed around the abandoned monastery. The enormous roots of a tree divided into sections and ran down a roof that was covered in weeds and vines and moss and all other kinds of unwanted plantation.

"Hello?" Oscar shouted. His voice rebounded back at him.

He stepped forward. A big spider ran past his leg, and he jumped.

What the hell was he doing here?

"Hello, is anyone there?"

Where was there to sleep? As far as he could tell, these rooms were open, damp and exposed. This wasn't a home; it was a mess. It had been left to rot for a reason.

"Hey, I just travelled ages to get here, it would be nice if someone actually came out and said hello!"

Nothing.

He threw his hands in the air and landed them on his hips. He turned, looking around, growing more and more frustrated.

Had this all just been for nothing?

He took out his phone. Dialled Lorenzo's number and put it to his ear.

The phone rang and rang until the answer machine answered.

"This is Father Lorenzo Romano, I can't get to the phone right now. If you would like to leave a message—"

Lorenzo's answer machine message stopped. Oscar

looked at his phone.

No signal.

"Dammit," he muttered, lifting the phone into the air.

He rotated, but no bars appeared. He kept spinning and turning, lifting his phone higher and higher — then halted.

A man stood in front of him. Bald head. Old. Robes that were probably once a clean white and a vibrant orange, now faded and tatty.

He watched Oscar with a knowing yet unassuming smile.

"Hey, are you Om Samsara?"

The man paused, then nodded a tiny nod.

"Great. Did Father Lorenzo Romano tell you I was coming?"

Another pause, and a tiny nod.

"Hey, do you speak or what?"

Another pause, then nothing. The man stayed still, watching him.

"Just fantastic," Oscar declared.

He huffed. Tried to stay calm.

"So I was told you defeated The Devil?"

Om shook his head. "I did not defeat him."

"You what?"

"I said I did not defeat him."

Oscar couldn't have heard that right.

"Did you just say you did not defeat him?"

"That is correct."

"Then what am I doing here?"

"I did not defeat him, I resisted him. I have this temple, and he cannot get me here. All I did was not give into my temptations."

"Yeah, right. See, I think I already have that part down."

"Do you?"

"Yeah, pretty much."

"Then you have no reason for being here, and you should

probably leave."

Oscar exhaled a large, angry sigh and threw his arms in the air.

"This is bullshit," he said.

He'd had enough.

He was so very, very close to exploding. He had travelled all this way for nothing. This was ridiculous.

He picked up his phone again and went to dial Lorenzo's number.

The man moved in such a sudden motion that Oscar didn't quite know what to do — he had met no one who looked this old and moved so quickly. Om was so quick, in fact, that Oscar could do nothing to stop him from grabbing the phone from Oscar's hand.

"What is this?" Om asked.

"It's an iPhone, give it back."

"What does it do?"

"Everything, pretty much."

Om smiled at Oscar, a friendly, *thank you for explaining* smile — then threw the phone on the ground, smashing it beyond use.

"Are you kidding me?" Oscar snapped, rushing to pick up the phone.

The screen had come off in tiny pieces. The inside was bent. The battery was scraped.

"Now I don't have any way of checking on April," Oscar said.

"That matters to you?" Om asked.

"Stop answering everything I say with a question!"

"You don't like questions?"

"I don't like people smashing my phone."

"Because you need your phone?"

"Because it is *my* phone."

"And that is important to you?"

"Shut. Up!"

Oscar turned around. He had no way of phoning a taxi, and no way of looking at Google Maps to see where he was. He was screwed.

"Why did you do that?" he demanded, turning back to Om.

"Is that what you mean to ask?"

"What? Yes, it is. The question I am asking is why you smashed my phone."

"You are asking the right question, but in the wrong way."

"Oh, because I'm shouting?"

"It has nothing to do with shouting."

"Just please tell me why you smashed my phone."

"Your phone?"

"Yes."

"You don't need it."

"I need it to keep in contact with home."

"Home?"

"Yes. With my friends."

"Friends?"

"Stop that!"

He jabbed his finger at Om and realised his entire body had tensed. He felt his cheeks reddening, and his arms shaking.

"My friend," Om said. "I see no chance of you defeating Mara. You cling onto too much of this world and are so against the other."

Oscar waved him away and turned. Looked around. He couldn't head back yet; he would have to stay the night. But where exactly?

"Maybe you should give up," Om continued. "I heard you've already done that once. Maybe you can give up again. And again, and again, and again…"

"What is this?" Oscar said. "I mean, what are you on

about? Are you trying to teach me some mystical lesson? I've had better mentors than this who have taught me lessons without needing to act like a–"

"A what?"

"I travelled a long way to find you. Do you know that?"

"Travelled?"

"I said stop that."

"Again, you do not understand. You measure your journey in hours, I imagine?"

"Yeah. And money."

"Money?"

"Well, I should have seen that coming…"

He looked Om up and down. He hated how he looked so smug, yet, at the same time, not smug at all.

"So you're telling me you haven't even defeated The Devil?" Oscar asked.

"I defeat Mara every day."

"I mean, literally defeating him."

"There is no defeat."

Oscar sighed. He had a pounding headache.

"This is why you lose," Om said. "You give into temptation. You own this world, so it owns you."

"Oh, is that what it is? Thanks, now I can go back and win."

He walked toward the rooms, looking around. They were all comprised of stony, damp floors and cracked walls.

"I can't leave now," Oscar said. "I'm knackered, and it's late. Do you have a bed or anything? Somewhere I can sleep?"

Om raised his arms.

"What is that supposed to mean?" Oscar asked.

"Home is all around you. Sleep wherever you wish."

Om turned and walked away, leaving Oscar stumped.

This was a huge mistake.

14

From his bag, Oscar took out his hoody and a few t-shirts. He laid his clothes out on the least stony bit of ground to create a makeshift pillow. It was hot, so a duvet wasn't essential — but it was also raining. A few drips fell from the cracks between the stones above him, but the shelter kept most of him dry.

He hadn't expected to get much sleep, but he was so fatigued from the travelling and the walking that he eventually fell into a light slumber.

He awoke a few times, but never fully. He would open his eyes, remember where he was, and return to a vacant sleep.

It was in these moments, however, somewhere between asleep and awake, that they came to him.

Three women. Each of them beautiful. Each with brown skin, long, black hair, and lusciously vibrant robes loosely fastened around their perfect bodies.

The first approached him with something his body was severely lacking: water. She took Oscar's head, rested it on her lap, and held an aged cup over his lips. She felt warm, the material of her robes soft, and her lap was welcoming. As he lay on her, he felt himself feeling happier, feeling less lost.

She pressed the cup against his lips and poured. He drank.

It felt like water, but better. Like it was the cleanest water; clean in a way our rivers no longer are. He was refreshed. Hydrated. And she smelt so good.

She smiled down at him. He wanted her. Not just sexually, but for comfort. He wanted her body against his, her arms around him, and he wanted to feel her closeness forever.

She whispered, her lips barely moving, but the silent words travelling succinctly to Oscar's ears.

"We serve at your feet, master."

She moved away, and Oscar reached his arm out for her, begging her not to go.

But then the second one came.

She knelt beside him. Took his head on her lap and spoke without moving her lips.

"You hate the world, don't you, Oscar?"

"I do."

"You hate your friends, don't you, Oscar?"

"Always."

"You hate April. You hate everything about her. Don't you?"

"I hate her."

She lowered her forehead to his and allowed him to relish her closeness.

She left, and as he reached out for her, the third and final woman took her place, just as beautiful and desirable as the others.

She said nothing. She opened her hand, and beneath her robe was gold. Enough of it to keep him happy.

But, seeing that this was not what Oscar sought, she opened her other robe, and revealed April.

Her face. Alive. Healthy.

He leant up and reached out for her. Attached himself to the image. Kept it for himself. Refused to let anyone else near it.

And, as she stepped away, Oscar lay back on the ground that didn't feel so uncomfortable anymore.

The first one stroked her hand down his cheek, the tips of her fingers providing a soft sensation

The second kissed him, a gentle press against his lips.

The third mounted him.

She took her robes down her left shoulder, then down the right.

He desired her more than he had ever desired anything. Never mind this world, never mind fighting Mara — he had to touch her, had to feel her, had to be inside of her.

"Leave!" boomed a male voice.

Each woman looked up, startled, and backed away."No!" Oscar cried.

"Go!" boomed the voice again.

"Don't make them leave!"

Oscar leapt to his feet.

Om stood in the doorway, the moonlight hidden behind him.

The first woman vanished.

"No!"

Oscar reached out for the second woman, who also vanished.

Oscar ran up to Om and swung his fists. Om backed up, staying out of reach.

The third woman vanished.

Oscar stopped swinging. Fell still. Looked over his shoulder at where the women had been.

What had just happened?

Who were they? How had they done that?

Oscar turned back to Om, startled that he had tried to assault an old man.

"I'm so sorry," Oscar said.

"I don't have time to wait for you to grow up," Om said. "Come with me."

Om turned and left.

Oscar looked back over his shoulder once again, then followed.

15

OSCAR AND OM SAT OPPOSITE EACH OTHER, CROSS-LEGGED.

Om passed Oscar a bowl of rice, and Oscar ate it quickly. He felt desperately hungry. And, despite the woman having given him water, he felt so, so thirsty.

"Did you drink from her?"

Oscar nodded. Om looked downwards, disappointed.

"You are a fool," he said, handing over a bottle of water. "You will be even thirstier now. Drink this."

"I don't understand. If she let me drink, how am I thirstier?"

"The more of her thirst you quench, the thirstier you become."

"That doesn't make sense."

"Just drink."

Oscar drank a huge gulp of water, then finished his rice. Once he'd finished, he put the bowl down and looked at Om inquisitively.

"Was that real?" he asked.

"Depends what you mean by real."

"Were they actually there, or was it in my head?"

"Both. And neither."

"Please stop doing this, I am trying to understand."

"Then listen."

"I am listening, I–"

"No, you are asking questions. You cannot listen when you are talking."

"Fine."

Oscar waited. Om took a while, but Oscar forced himself to be patient, and waited for Om to speak.

"It is said that Mara tried to tempt Buddha, not just once, but many times, and in many ways. One way he tried to do so was with his daughters. His beautiful temptresses."

"You are telling me that was The Devil's daughters?"

"What did I say about asking questions?"

Oscar stopped speaking.

"Mara has three daughters. But what you need to understand about Mara, and everything he commands, is that he is not a physical being as you believe him to be."

"But I–"

Oscar stopped himself.

"Yes, you saw him in Hell, and yes, he is physically inhabiting April. But he is in all of us already. As are his daughters."

Oscar repeated Om's words to himself, trying to make sense of it all. He was struggling, but he tried.

"Each daughter comes from the folly of men. They prompt man to commit evil, just as Mara does through his existence in all of us. His first daughter is Tanha. She is thirst."

Oscar nodded. Yes, that made sense. The first woman quenched Oscar's thirst — he was desperate for water, a feeling that came on suddenly, and she let him drink. Yet he still felt more dehydrated afterwards.

"The second daughter, Arati, is aversion and discontentment."

Arati, who had tried to make Oscar hate everything.

He remembered what she had said. That he hated his friends. That he hated this world.

That I hated April.

Was that true? That he hated his friends? He knew he hadn't treated them very well recently, but he didn't think he hated them... and he certainly did not hate April. He loved April more than he loved anything.

How had they manipulated him so well?

"And the third and final daughter is Raga — she is attachment. She is desire. She is greed."

She had shown Oscar wealth. When that failed, she showed Oscar the only thing he was attached to: April.

It made sense.

He went to speak, then stopped himself.

"You can ask your question; I imagine it's the right one."

"Okay... How did they manipulate me so easily? How did they turn me against what I believe? I don't understand."

"These women offer relief and temptation, and that is what you are after. They appear because they try to tempt you. They are hypnotic."

"They hypnotised me?"

"In a way."

"How did they not hypnotise you?"

Om smiled. "That is the right question."

Oscar waited for him to answer it.

"Yet," Om continued, "if you ask that question, you won't find the answer."

"What?"

"To be hypnotised, you require the perception that you can be hypnotised. Look around me. I have nothing. I want nothing. How could they offer me temptation when there is nothing to tempt me? You need to let go of your illusion of self, Oscar. You are no one."

"I am no one?"

"Not in the way you say it, with that angry look on your face. You are no one in the most glorious sense of the phrase."

Om stood.

"Where are you going?"

"Rest, Oscar. It is late. They won't attack again tonight. We will continue in the morning."

Om went to leave, then paused by the doorway, and turned back.

"Oh, and by the way," he said. "If Mara is sending his daughters to you, that is because he knows you are here. It is an aggressive act on his part. The war is getting tougher."

Om left, leaving Oscar on his own.

As Om's parting words grew clear, he realised that meant things were about to get much tougher for Thea and Henry back at home.

16

It was beans on toast for tea. Thea wished she could be more inventive, but she was hesitant to go out food shopping as it would mean leaving Henry on his own. Henry could do it, but then again, she didn't particularly wish to be left alone either.

So, beans on toast it was.

Fortunately, she had found a tin of beans that had the little sausages in too. A small pleasure in a big, nasty world.

She and Henry ate in silence.

The ceiling continued to shake and pound and rattle until — until it didn't.

Until a silence descended, and they could momentarily think again. Like the eye of the storm, showing a little sunshine before the terror persisted.

But that wasn't it. It wasn't a gap, nor was it rest — it was something more.

Thea felt it.

Something had changed. Shifted. Twisted somehow.

The thing upstairs had not stopped because it lost power.

Quite the opposite. It had stopped because it was gaining power, and would soon be able to do more than just make noise.

Henry looked at her, almost optimistic. But her eyes were widening, drifting slowly upwards, and his optimism faded as her dread became clear.

"What is it?" he asked.

She stood. Not deliberately; she had made no conscious decision to elevate herself upwards, but she did.

"Thea, what is–"

She raised a hand to silence him and waited.

Listened.

She was an exorcist and a conduit. A powerful Sensitive. Things changing didn't get past her. She used to think it was noise in her brain, that it was meaningless madness — but she understood now that it wasn't madness, it was the truth; the answers.

"Something has changed," she said, so quietly she wasn't sure Henry had heard it.

But he had. He rose to his feet too.

"What?" he asked. "What's changed?"

She hesitated. They needed to go up there. Both of them; she wasn't going alone. But then what?

She couldn't just leave it.

She had to go see for herself.

But she dreaded doing so…

She walked to the wall and reached up to a crucifix hanging on a nail. She took it down, held it in front of her, and willed herself to reconsider.

She couldn't. She had promised Oscar. She owed this to April.

"Come on," she said, and wandered out of the room.

She edged to the first step, placing her foot on it and

listening to its gentle creak. Her next foot moved to the next step, and she paused again.

She was powerful. More so than any Sensitive. So why was she so afraid?

She looked back at Henry.

Because what's up there is even more powerful than I am...

Henry looked terrified, and she realised her fear was infecting him. She tried to present a calm face, a relaxed posture, a smile.

She was unconvincing.

She proceeded up the next few steps, and the next few again, until she found herself on the landing.

The door to the room was marginally open.

She had not done that.

Oscar had said that it would soon be strong enough to break free of its restraints. She wondered how long it would be until it had the power to release itself.

She took a deep breath. Edged forward, holding the crucifix out, feeling Henry's awkward presence behind her.

What if it was waiting for her behind the door? Ready to pounce as soon as she walked in? Was she about to die?

She muttered a prayer under her breath, hoping it would provide her some kind of protection, however little it may offer against something so strong.

"Father, I come to You today, bowing in my heart, asking for protection from sin."

She reached her hand out.

"Set our minds on You."

She placed her palm on the door.

"Help us by the power of Your Spirit."

She pushed the door, and it scraped open.

"Let us be invincible to the evil one."

"Is that what they call me?" it said. "The evil one?"

There it was. Still on the bed. Still in restraints. Still destroying April's body and leering back at Thea.

She looked around. Nothing seemed to have changed. There was more power, but it didn't appear to have achieved much.

She edged in, not averting her eyes from it for a second. Henry hovered in the doorway.

"What are you doing?" Thea asked.

"What can I do?"

"You don't fool me."

"Fool you?"

"I know you're stronger than this."

"My dear, when I am strong enough to free myself from this bed, I assure you, I will. And it will not be long."

Was it a lie? Was what she felt wrong? Had it not grown in power?

"You're going to lose," Thea said defiantly. "You disgusting little—"

A jolt of her body followed a quick slice of pain across her chest, and she fell to her knees, coughing.

She pushed herself up. Ran out of the room. Slammed the door behind her, pounded down the stairs, fell to her knees.

She panted. She still felt it. It was a searing, awful pain.

She lifted her top.

From above her left breast to her right hip was a slit. An open wound, blood trickling out. Like a claw had dug into the surface of her skin and dragged itself downwards.

She covered her chest up again, ignoring the patch of blood appearing through her top.

"What is it?" Henry asked.

Should she let him see it? Would it not scare him more?

It could not do that yesterday. Or even an hour ago.

Henry looked expectantly at her, and she had nothing to say.

She was in charge. She had to lead him. She had to make the decisions. But all she could think about was how much she dreaded what was to come, and begged for Oscar to hurry.

17

"LET ME ASK YOU A QUESTION FOR A CHANGE," OM SAID, walking studiously around the outskirts of the temple with his hands behind his back.

Oscar followed, hands in his pockets. They were walking casually, yet they were striding. He couldn't decide whether to relax and saunter, or hurry to keep up.

"Is evil an intrinsic characteristic or an external force?" Om asked.

"What do you mean?"

"As in, is evil something within all of us, or is it something that comes from outside and attacks us?"

"It's something from outside. All humanity can do evil, but grand acts of evil require an intervention with divine evil. It is something that attacks us."

"Is it?"

"Why, what do you think it is?"

Om stopped. Stood upon a large stone overlooking the forest. Oscar stopped too, looking over the beautiful view. He wondered how difficult it was for Om, never being able to leave this temple, but seeing what beauty there was beyond it.

Then again, the guy didn't seem discontented. He didn't appear to want to leave. He had no use for the world beyond his home. Om had already been keen to emphasise that he owned nothing.

"Prince Siddhartha was once approached by Mara."

"Prince Siddhartha?"

"Buddha."

"Ah."

"Mara approached with the appearance of having the prince's interests. His aim was to give him what he was tempted by, what he felt he needed, to weaken his resolve. Do you know what the prince said?"

"What?"

"He recognised who Mara was. He said he saw Mara's troops around him and that, even if the rest of the world could not defeat Mara's army, he would defeat it with wisdom."

"That's all great, but wisdom doesn't really defeat the mass of demons possessing all these victims."

"You think Buddha was referring to Mara's demons when he referred to his troops?"

"You think he wasn't?"

Om took one of his many pauses where he would take a breath, look around, and appear to contemplate his next words.

"Condemning someone or something as evil is counter-productive. It implies it is okay to do them harm."

"If I perform an exorcism, I will do it to cause that demon harm. How else will I do it?"

"That is your problem. Do not aim to fight the demon; instead, aim to free the victim."

"But I don't under–"

"Watch this."

Om pointed to the leaf on a nearby tree. Attached to it was a spider's web, with a large spider that made Oscar shudder. Oscar did not like spiders, and he went to turn away.

"Watch," Om said, and Oscar unwillingly turned his head back.

A fly of some kind had been trapped in the web. The spider crawled across its web, reaching the fly, and spread its mouth over the fly's head. Within minutes, the fly was eaten.

Oscar grimaced.

"Why did that spider eat the fly?" Om asked.

"I don't know.

"Yes, you do."

Oscar shrugged. "Because it is in its nature, maybe? To survive. Or instinct."

"So you do not consider the spider evil?"

"I guess not."

"Because it is in its nature?"

"Yes."

Om smiled.

"What?" Oscar said.

"Do you really not see the point I am making?"

"All I see is a spider eating a fly."

"Which is in its nature. Yet, what if Mara ate the fly? Is that because it is in Mara's nature, or because Mara is evil?"

"I–"

Oscar went to respond, but realised he had no response.

Om turned once again, continued walking, and Oscar followed. Om allowed the silence to linger, giving a chance for the lesson to become clear — but Oscar was struggling to comprehend exactly what Om was saying.

Oscar sighed. The more he thought about the answers, the more he hated the questions.

"To answer my earlier question," he said, "as to whether

evil is an intrinsic characteristic or an external force — why can it not be both? You fight that demon with aggression, and that cannot work."

"Why not?"

"Evil can only weaken a lesser evil. But Mara is the strongest evil there is — there is no evil greater. And aggression can only come from evil. So how do you expect to defeat Mara with it?"

"So what am I supposed to do?"

"Defeat evil with good — something you have never done before. You must let go of what you perceive to be evil and relieve yourself of the burden of belief."

"What belief?"

"The belief that Mara is something to be angry with."

Oscar stopped walking. He huffed, hands on his hips, and looked over the view, frustrated and annoyed. He knew there was a lesson in there, but it all just sounded like words, and he had a continuous headache that was only getting bigger.

Om kept walking a few paces then, when he realised Oscar was not with him, he stopped.

"I can't look at something evil without knowing how evil it is," Oscar said.

"You are attached to your perceptions, as much as you are attached to your anger toward your friends. This is Mara's work. You must let go of it if you are to stand a chance."

"But The Devil *is* evil. How am I supposed to just pretend he's not?"

"Because it is not up to you to make such a judgement."

"This is ridiculous."

Om said nothing. He watched Oscar, not perturbed or annoyed, just curious — then walked on.

Oscar hurried to catch up.

"So I should let go of everything that makes me human?" he asked, unable to hide the annoyance in his voice.

"No, you should let go of everything that has Mara's influence. Whether it be memories, beliefs, experiences or people that force you to hold on to your anger; you have to let them go. It takes someone who is truly divine to defeat Mara."

"I'm not holding onto anger."

"Aren't you?"

"No! I am not! I mean, I wish things could be different, but I'm not angry."

"Then tell me of a person, past or present, who you consider yourself to not be angry with?"

Oscar went to speak, but found he could not answer.

He was mad at Julian for being so condescending. For hating him for loving April, for always having to ruin happy moments with truth.

He was mad at his parents for being mad at him. He hated them for never believing that he was being bullied as a child. He hated them for their disappointment in his lack of ambition as a teenager, and their unwillingness to accept his chosen career.

He was mad at April for going into Hell to rescue him. He was mad at Lacy for letting her. He was mad at Henry for not going home like the rest of the recruits. And he was mad at Thea, but to be honest, he wasn't even sure why.

"Have you just thought about all the people you are mad at?"

Oscar rolled his eyes. "Yeah, I have."

"And I bet not one of them was Mara. Your devil."

Oscar went to object, but thought — Om was right. He hadn't.

"He is the one who's caused all this torment, and yet you direct your anger at your friends."

"But I–"

"That anger you have against Mara rules all of your

307

emotions. That is why you can't let go of the perception. Yet, if you keep it up, you may find yourself hating your way to losing everything."

They walked onwards but did not speak.

They didn't need to. Oscar already had so much to reflect on.

18

Oscar needed a break away from Om to think, so he took a walk outside the temple, through the forest. All around him trees hugged each other, animals sang their mating calls, and life flourished in its absence of humankind.

It wasn't easy, being forced to question himself. He didn't believe that he always made the right decision, of course he didn't — but he believed he tried.

But to say that he was fuelling the Mara within, that he was feeding the evil inside, that he was battling The Devil with The Devil's own creations...

Maybe it just showed how clever his opponent was. He wasn't just a master of evil, but a master of manipulation, bringing out the characteristics in Oscar that The Devil knew would mean he had no chance.

But how was Oscar supposed to change? What, was he supposed to just let go of a lifetime of resentment? To suddenly not care about the torment he faced in childhood, the battles he'd engaged with, the demons that had tormented him. Bertrand, Hayley, Father O'Neil — was he meant to be stop being angry at them?

Honestly, he did not know if he could. He'd spent such a long time harnessing this anger, and using it to fuel his victories, that he did not know how he was supposed to stop it from affecting him.

Was he really that angry?

He decided, right there and then, that he would not be angry, or jealous, or envious, or resentful, or ungrateful. He closed his eyes and told himself the world was good, that The Devil did not deserve his judgement, that...

He failed.

He looked to his feet, shaking his head. The tension in his body grew. His biceps tightened, his breathing quickened, his legs shook.

April had given birth to a child that had systematically destroyed their lives. Hayley, or Lamia as she was truly called, had controlled him, influenced him, and made him almost kill April. Was he supposed to forgive that demon for almost destroying the life they had built?

Father O'Neil had appeared as a mentor, disguising the demon that had amalgamated years before they met. He manipulated Julian, April and Oscar into a temporary absence from this world, and brought on its end in doing so. Was he supposed to pretend that this mess would not have been created had O'Neil not been successful? That his bringing forth the demons of Hell had not prompted thousands of deaths?

What of the demon that forced Julian to slice his own throat? Was he supposed to pretend that had never happened?

And now, at that very moment, The Devil was destroying April. April was probably in agonising torture, simply because she tried to rescue Oscar.

Oscar's anger fuelled him. It gave him strength. It powered him. It drove him forward in this battle — it was his motivation. It was the reason he was here; the reason he was listening Om's lessons. And now he was not only being told to let it go, but to avoid acknowledging that The Devil was evil?

His body tensed, the anger grew, and he swung his fist at a nearby tree.

Stupid move. Now his fist hurt, and his skin was cracked.

Another silly wound created by a silly action.

He paused by a tree stump. Sat on it. Looked up at the branches blocking out the blue sky.

He was so very far away from home. It was so peaceful. Animals lived their lives untouched by the destruction of mankind. Oscar wondered what this forest would look like after The Devil had set it alight. The fire would spread quickly through the trees, destroying the untouched beauty with little care for the life it harnessed.

Oscar lost track of time, sitting there, thinking about the world he had come to hate, amongst part of the world he could grow to love. He knew he should return, that time was limited, and Om probably had many more complicated philosophies to share.

He just didn't want to return.

He wanted to stay here.

If April was beside him, he would. They would wait until dark, hand in hand, saying nothing.

Words could never say what silence could.

It reminded him what he was fighting for. If he could save the world, then great — but it was April he needed. It always was.

But it was his attachment to April that made him hate The Devil.

He huffed.

Why did this all have to fall on him?

A decade ago, he'd be finishing his shift behind the supermarket checkouts, returning home, and shutting away the world. He would close his curtains, put on his Xbox, and refuse to acknowledge that anyone else existed.

He'd wished for something greater, now he wished for something simpler.

A year later, he and April were in their own home, and she was pregnant.

He froze that memory, not allowing his thoughts to continue any further through time, like his mind had taken a picture and he was watching it develop.

If he kept his eyes closed, he could pretend that nothing else had ever happened, and that there was nothing for him to be angry about.

But denial was of no use to his situation. He had to return to the temple where Om would be waiting for him, ready to tell him he was wrong for holding on so tightly to thoughts that did nothing but torture him.

OSCAR LAY IN BED — OR, AT LEAST, SOMETHING RESEMBLING A bed. His clothes were piled upon the stone, and he was trying to ignore the bumps in his back.

All the day's conversations were just starting to settle in on him, and he was attempting to make some clarity out of it. He had spent the day getting less frustrated as things began to make sense, then more frustrated when they no longer did; like he was on a constant pendulum that slowed down then sped up whenever it felt like it.

He had spent the rest of that day learning about Buddha's Four Noble Truths.

Om had told him that there was the truth of suffering, the truth of the cause of suffering, truth of the end of suffering, and truth of the path that led to the end of suffering.

"Suffering exists," Om had told him. "It has a cause, but it also has an end, but it has a cause to bring about its end."

Oscar had made Om pause so he could repeat those words to himself.

"That's a bit miserable, isn't it?" he'd objected.

"I can understand why you may see it that way, but it is

not intended to create a negative worldview. Instead, it is an acceptance of the world as it is, and that acceptance allows us to rectify it. It is a contingency plan to deal with the suffering humanity faces."

"And what is that plan?"

"Karma."

"Karma? Isn't that the idea that bad things happen to someone who's bad? I thought you said bad didn't exist?"

"Finally, you are asking the right questions. That is not the real concept of Karma, it is how you in the west have interpreted it."

"So what is Karma then?"

"It is cause and effect. The idea that things are because things have been. But if this is true, it also means that things are because things will be. And those causes you still have control over."

Even now, as he rested, going over those words again and again, Oscar was still struggling to understand.

There was no evil, yet he'd been fighting evil his entire life.

There was suffering because it has been caused, and it will end.

Things are because of cause and therefore cause can...

He ran his hands over his head. He'd lost himself again.

He tried to quiet his mind. Leave the thoughts until tomorrow. They could wait for him to rest. He was so tired.

He went inside his bag and pulled out the one thing he could not do without.

A picture. Sunny day. He was in it, but he was not the focus.

The focus was on the beautiful, vibrant being next to him. The woman that he has done everything for. The woman for which he fought. She looked so different to how he'd left her. So healthy. So alive.

Nothing destroying her from the inside.

He wondered how much she was suffering. How much it hurt. How much she could endure before she begged for mercy.

Those thoughts weren't helpful. He willed them away, and just focussed on the picture. On the April he knew.

He closed his eyes, held onto that thought, and kept it with him until he fell asleep.

20

Henry slept in a sleeping bag, on an airbed, on the floor of Thea's room. The spare room was ready for him, with fresh sheets and plenty of space, but he did not wish to use it. He could not bear to be on his own and, even though Thea hadn't said it, he had a feeling Thea couldn't either.

In a strange, unexpected way, they missed the noises. Those clatters and bangs and rumbles of the ceiling that terrified them had stopped and, in the silence, they found a far more unsettling kind of terror. An eerie sense that something was wrong, but they did not know what.

Before, they knew that it was there and what it was doing. Now they had no idea.

For all they knew, it had broken free and was walking along the hallway at that very moment, edging closer, ready to open that bedroom door and slice their throats in their sleep.

Henry kept his eyes focussed on that door.

Staring.

Not looking away, not allowing himself a moment of freedom.

It did not open, nor did it move, nor did it creak.

He knew he would not get any sleep. Not while he was staring at the door. But he was too afraid to look away.

He unzipped the sleeping bag. Stood. Looked at Thea. She lay with her back to him, but there were no deep breaths that might signal sleep, and he was sure she was just as awake.

He said nothing to her. To share their fear with each other would make the threat too real. Keeping it unspoken, much like the silence that haunted them, meant they could leave it to fester beneath the surface, unacknowledged.

He edged toward the window. Looked outside. The night was silent and still. The branches of the tree did not wave in the wind, and the blades of grass did not brush in the breeze. It was an empty night, void of the living or the dead.

Or so he thought. He saw a brief flicker of something; a movement in the distance.

That movement could have been anything. A shadow, a cat, a person stumbling home drunk.

But chances were, if there was something there, it wasn't just anything. It would be *some*thing.

He urged himself to stop fearing the worse.

But the movement came closer. The silhouette of a person became vaguely visible from the distance.

The person was walking. It was a steady walk where each step was like the last; almost robotic, but more demented.

It was a man. Pale faced. Dead-eyed.

He stopped outside the house.

"Thea," Henry prompted.

She stirred.

"Thea, come here."

She pushed the covers off. He kept his eyes on this man.

Another person appeared. A woman. Skinny, her posture slumped, her face empty.

A child emerged to the right. Smeared red cheeks. Bruised eyes.

Each of these people paused, metres from the house. Watching. Not moving closer, but not walking away. Hovering, absentmindedly.

Thea arrived at Henry's side.

"What's happening?"

She rubbed her eyes, but her grogginess quickly left. She looked from one figure to the other, then peered into the distance to see if she could see any more.

"Shit," she unknowingly muttered.

"Do you think they will try to come in?" Henry asked.

"No," Thea said. "At least, I don't think so. Not yet."

"Not yet?"

"They are not here to attack."

"Then what are they here for?"

Thea looked over her shoulder at the door. Listened to the silence. Waited for some movement that would indicate that *it* was stirring.

Nothing.

"Thea?" Henry prompted, his voice fraught with fear.

"They are here for him," Thea said.

"They've come to collect him?"

"No. No one needs to collect The Devil."

"Then what?"

"They are followers. Disciples. Come for guidance. To worship. To protect."

"What does that mean?"

"It means they know."

"Know what?"

"That it's almost time. That *he* is almost ready to escape."

21

Om gave Oscar a pear.

Oscar stared at it and waited for the rest of his meal.

Om did not notice. He bit into his pear, its juices running down his cheek, and appeared to take neither pleasure nor displeasure from it.

"This it?" Oscar said.

Om took out another pear and passed it to him.

This man was both remarkable and infuriating. Oscar had grown up expecting milk and cereal for breakfast, sandwiches, fruit and cake for lunch, and a substantial meal for tea, rarely having the same thing two days in a row. This man took what he needed from the environment and did not complain. He never showed hunger, nor boredom. He always seemed content without showing much of anything.

Oscar bit into the pear. It was a good pear, but it was unlikely to keep him satisfied until tea — and who knew what they'd have for tea. More pears, probably.

Oscar snorted at his inward joke and took a larger bite. Om did not react.

He finished his pear and, before beginning the other one, aimed an inquisitive look at Om.

"Do you know what's been bugging me?"

"I know nothing."

Oscar ignored the response, despite it not really making sense.

"You call it Mara. We call it The Devil. In Islam it's Iblis, in Hindu it's, what, Kali?"

Om continued eating, awaiting the question.

"Well, how do we know we are all talking about the same thing? How do we know this thing I've faced, that's inside April, is the thing I call The Devil, you call Mara, and whoever calls whatever?"

He took another bite and finished the pear.

"And," he continued, "on that point, if we are not all talking about the same thing, then who is right? Is it Mara, is it The Devil — what is it?"

"You think a lot."

Oscar was perturbed. "I thought you'd encourage me to think. Isn't that the point of you answering all my questions with a question?"

"We all have our interpretations. It matters not what we call them or how they are represented. What matters is that we all know it as one's perception of evil, and that we can recognise its temptations."

"So, I mean, how is Mara presented to you? I mean, what does he look like?"

"He is depicted as a warlord, mounted on an elephant, with a legion of troops."

"See, I've always seen him as this bloke with devil horns. In fact, that is what he looks like — I saw it when I confronted him."

"That's how he *presented* himself when you confronted him."

"What's that meant to mean?"

"To you, his legion of troops are the demons you face, each of them representing a sin. To me, the troops are figurative — such as restlessness, doubt, wrath. We must fight off the demons inside of us."

"Yeah, but I have actually faced these demons."

"Who was the first?"

"What?"

"The first demon you faced. Who was it?"

Oscar cast his mind back to all those years ago, when he was confronted with little Kaylee Kemple, a child with nothing innocent about her. A demon possessed her, and he would never forget its name.

"It was Ardat Lili."

"Ardat Lili is a succubus, yes?"

"She is."

"She is a demon who comes to men at night and uses them to impregnate her with demon spawn."

"That's accurate."

"So that evil is infidelity. It's sexual temptation. Men fight that evil often, although rarely is it in a tangible form like you fought."

"But I did fight it."

"Even then, it was inside a girl. You did not see the demon yourself, correct?"

"I guess."

"Then, for all you know, you were fighting the sin, not the demon."

"In a little girl?"

"Who says the girl was the one sinning?"

Oscar ran his hands over his face. Another headache.

"Buddha sees these things as diversions from his goal of freedom," Om said. "You must let go of all things you are attached to in order to resist their temptation."

"So I shouldn't be worried about my girlfriend? I should just let go of her?"

"What did you just call her?"

"What, my girlfriend?"

Om took a big breath and nodded, as if Oscar had just walked into a trap he wasn't aware of.

"You refer to her as *my* girlfriend."

"Yes."

"Once you stop referring to things with *me* or *my* or *mine*, you will no longer be influenced. If Mara cannot influence you, that is how you beat it — but so long as you give into temptations you aren't even aware you're giving into, Mara will always be indestructible."

"So I should let go of the one I love?"

"You have been picked deliberately, and not just because you are a Sensitive and April is a conduit. While you think your love gives you strength, Mara uses it to give himself power."

"My love for April has always given me power."

"And the anger that love provokes has always given you weakness."

"So what do I do?"

Om paused.

"You let go of anything you do not wish to lose, meaning it cannot be taken from you and Mara cannot use it to win."

"But–"

"You think I beat Mara? That is why you are here, yes? I did not beat him, I merely resisted him. He tried to tempt me, and he couldn't because there is nothing to tempt me with. You will not stand a chance unless you have nothing he can use."

"But what is the point of me saving April if I let go of her?"

"Because he keeps using this against you. So long as he is

in April, he knows you will not fight him with everything you have, for risk of losing her. He is using her to provoke anger in you, to provoke jealousy, fury, envy — and that is why he wins. That is why he doesn't just kill her. Once you lose her, then you will have a power over him he cannot touch. Until then... he controls you."

"It seems wrong. It goes against the principles of every exorcism I've performed."

Om sighed. Hesitated. Dropped his head.

This was the closest to being frustrated Oscar had seen him yet.

But it was quick and short-lived. In seconds, he had returned to his calm self.

"Come," he demanded, and began striding across the temple. Oscar quickly pushed himself to his feet and followed.

22

OM STOOD AT THE EDGE OF THE TEMPLE BOUNDARIES, INCHES from a steep drop. As Oscar caught up, Om closed his eyes, took in the air that so gracefully filled his lungs, and let it go.

"Look around," he said.

Oscar looked around. A shitty temple and some forest. And what?

"Everything is interconnected. Everything is because other things are. The plants take in the carbon dioxide and give out the oxygen. We take in the oxygen and give out the carbon dioxide. We cannot exist without the other. It is a perfect combination that has taken billions of years to be perfected, yet is not perfect at all."

"Om, I don't understand what you're saying."

"Everything *is* — because other things *are*. What is happening now is because of what happened before and will provoke what happens next. There is no absolute; nothing exists independently. There is no self. Your personality changes for various people. Who you are is not who you are. You are nothing and everything."

"You're just babbling now."

"You are no one, and everyone."

"I am a Sensitive. I fight evil, that is my purpose, that is who I am."

"Let go of that notion and be what you are without needing to be something."

Oscar had absolutely no idea what that was meant to mean. It sounded like Om was just babbling cliché after cliché. His frustration bubbled, and a sudden image of April's broken, contorted face re-emerged into Oscar's thoughts, like a bolt of lightning shattering a precariously built house. He had thought he was learning something, but this was just nonsense. Just rambling. He needed to be home and be with her. He couldn't keep doing this.

He was wasting his time.

"I can't do this," Oscar decided. "I have to go."

Oscar turned to walk away.

"You still do not understand!" Om snapped.

Oscar waved him away with his hand. "I just don't have the time when The Devil is–"

Om grabbed Oscar by his jacket, put his face just next to his, and spoke with the most passion Oscar had heard him use so far.

"Mara isn't just The Devil. The Devil isn't just something that commands demons. It is something inside of us. It is the psychophysical existence, and the reason humans have to die is so we can kill that part of us off."

"I don't have that, I am a Sen–"

"Whoever you are, whether or not Heaven conceived you, it is impossible for you to survive without a little of Hell inside of you too. The nature of man must involve Mara. It is the agent of chaos that opposes the order of our minds. It is the nonduality of good and evil."

Om's passion faded. Slowly, his hand loosened its grip on Oscar's jacket, and he stood back. He used his arm to indicate all the trees and bushes and plants and bugs before them.

"Life is not the absence of Mara, but the constant conquering of him. We do it every day, and you have defeated The Devil for every minute you've been alive by not giving in to him, and April suffers because you accept that evil. All you're doing now is fuelling it so you can't defeat it again. You defeated Mara with smaller choices, only now your choices are bigger, and that makes it tougher — that is the only difference. Give me the picture."

"What?"

"Your picture. I know you hold on to it. It's in your pocket, give it to me."

"No."

"You want to beat Mara?"

"That's why I'm here for Christ's sake!"

"Then *give it to me!*"

Oscar took the picture of April out of his pocket and presented it.

"If you destroy this picture," Oscar said, "I will–"

"I am not going to destroy it." Om took the picture and pressed it against Oscar's chest. "You are."

"You are kidding me."

Oscar snatched the picture out of Om's reach and turned to walk away. Om went to grab Oscar's jacket, but Oscar knocked his arm out of the way this time. He marched away, only to hear Om's feet quickly following.

"This picture is not her, but it may as well be," Om called after him. "It provokes in you everything Mara wishes to use."

"This picture is the only thing keeping me going," Oscar said, not breaking his stride. "It is all that makes me suffer through your bullshit. She gives me this strength, that is why I have it."

"She does not give you strength, Oscar. She is the reason you can't seem to understand anything I say."

"Is she? Or is it because you're talking a load of crap!"

Om smiled. This annoyed Oscar more. He stopped and turned back to Om, jabbing his finger at his face.

"I am sick of this shit, and I am sick of you."

"All I did was ask you to tear up a picture, and this is how you react. Tell me, is that the good side of you? Or is this the side Mara will have provoked?"

"Oh, what, you're saying Mara made me do it?"

"His troops."

"Fuck his troops."

"Precisely."

"No, I..."

He looked down at the picture. April looked backed up at him, smiling that smile that let him know she loved him.

"You are attached to this picture because you are attached to its memory. I am not asking you to stop loving her, I am asking you to let go of the attachment that Mara continues to use."

"It isn't−"

"Tell me, Oscar. You confronted your devil in Hell, did you not?"

"Yes, I did," he said proudly, as if to gloat that this is something Om had never done.

"And you were winning at one point, were you not?"

"It felt like it."

"And at what point did you stop winning?"

"When April came back to save−"

He stopped talking.

He should have seen that one coming.

He dropped his head. Closed his eyes. It was true, should April not have tried to save him, he would have stood a much greater chance.

"You didn't win for the same reason she came down to save you," Om said, speaking slower now, seeing realisation dawning upon Oscar.

All of this evil would not have occurred had he and April never have fallen in love.

He went to save her, and the balance shifted, and demons threw themselves into the world.

She went to save him, and he could no longer defeat The Devil and send those demons back.

Om was right. The only way he could save her was by letting her go. She was the burden, the attachment that meant he could not win. All this anger he felt was because of the torment she was going through, and he had to stop that anger.

He was walking right into The Devil's trap. He was behaving just as The Devil wished.

That was why he was losing.

The only way to save her was to remove the attachment.

He looked at her face in the picture one last time, then ripped it in half. Then in half again. Then again. Then one final time.

He let the pieces go and, despite the calm day, a gust of wind pushed through and took the pieces into the sky, out of Oscar's reach.

23

OSCAR SLEPT WELL THAT NIGHT.

The makeshift bed was still uncomfortable, but that didn't matter. He had shelter and he had his clothes to rest his head on — which was more than many people had. He felt fortunate in a way that he hadn't before; he was less angry, less impatient, and more grateful.

His mind drifted into a dreamless sleep. The kind of sleep one only has when they are relaxed; when their mind is not fighting all the nasty images their subconscious tries to present.

But it didn't last long.

He heard it. The whisper. A woman's hushed voice.

His eyes opened.

And there she was. Beautiful, in her wondrous robes.

Oscar felt parched. So dehydrated. So desperate for water.

She took his head, rested its heavy weight upon her legs, and made it feel light. She brought the bottle to his lips and tilted it.

He wanted water so much. He needed it. His throat was

dry. He hadn't realised how thirsty he was, but now he did, he had to have some.

But, just as it touched his lips, he turned his face away.

His body may need it, but his mind did not.

He took his head from her lap and pushed himself back.

He wanted so much to touch her, to taste her.

No, I don't, he told himself.

He didn't need her, and he didn't need her water.

But he still didn't run away. He stayed on his knees, allowing her to move to his side once again.

She placed the water at his lips.

He wanted to drink it so much. Just one swig would cure the dryness of his throat, a throat that felt like it had been scraped by sandpaper.

"Just drink…" she said, her voice dreamy, a harmonious whisper breathed against his ear. "Take it…"

He reached his hand up and placed it on her face. Just one sip, that was all he'd have, just one sip.

One sip and then the dry throat, the thirst, the desperation for water would end. He would be cured. Replenished.

But he did not. He closed his eyes and dropped his head, felt the flask against his lips. In a momentary burst of confidence, he punched the bottle away.

When he opened his eyes, she was gone, and the second woman was at Oscar's side, stroking his hair, smiling at him in a way that felt so comforting.

"It's okay, it's okay," she insisted. "You don't have to drink. You don't have to do anything. You don't have to listen to him."

"Him?"

"The monk. He lies. Everyone lies. I hate liars."

Oscar hated liars.

"Julian should not have left you."

Julian was a bastard for what he did.

"And The Devil is destroying everything."

The Devil was destroying everything.

"It is his fault, not yours. It is never yours."

It was.

What was Oscar thinking, listening to Om? The Devil was not responsible for his anger; Oscar was responsible, and him alone. He could not–

Stop it!

This was what she wanted.

He gazed up at her. She was so sweet, so beautiful, so loving, shining like a light that would burn all the bad thoughts away.

"You are so angry. You are right to be angry."

He sat up decisively. He had to fight it.

Om wasn't a liar.

He didn't hate Julian.

And he had grown to feel indifferent to The Devil. Despite the torment he had, he had allowed it. He was responsible too.

"Get away," he demanded.

He pushed her, and she backed off.

Then the third and final woman moved forward, and the others seemed to disappear from his eyeline. He could do nothing about this one — no resistance at all. She stood before him, her hair long, curling over her shoulders, her lips soft.

She took down her robes and presented the softest skin, a naked torso, her breasts petite and pointed. Oscar wanted to touch her. He wanted to take her, to be inside of her, feel what she was like. She was more than any man would want.

She was perfect.

She glided forward. Moved to her knees, crouching over Oscar, running her gentle fingers down his coarse, unshaven cheek.

"It's okay," she said. "You can take me. It will make you feel better."

It would make him feel better.

It would make him feel much, much better.

To be inside of her, to feel that moment of relief, that pleasure, those seconds of ecstasy. Maybe he should just do it for a bit of clarity, to close his mind. It had been a while since he and April had been able to be intimate, and she wouldn't know.

"Touch me," she whispered.

He reached out his hand, moving it toward her breast, his fingers outstretched.

But he did not touch her.

She moved forward, hoping to meet his fingers with her skin.

He retracted his hand.

She was godly. She was desirable. She was sex.

But she was not real.

He did not give in.

"Go," he said, weakly.

She leant over him, her eyes wilting, her lips pouting.

"I want you so bad…"

She can't have been lying. She must want him badly. Maybe there wasn't anything wrong with just a moment of–

Stop it!

"Go," he tried again, with stronger conviction.

She reached out, her hand on his leg, on his thigh, moving upwards.

"*Go!*"

He turned, closed his eyes, and willed them away. Refuted the temptation. Denied the feel of her touch or the words of comfort or the water he could have drunk.

He waited, listening to the heaviness of his breaths, waiting for the storm in his mind to die down.

When he looked up, they were gone.

And, in a moment of realisation, it all became clear. He realised why he hadn't defeated The Devil in Hell as prophesied. Why it hadn't worked.

And he finally knew what he had to do.

24

Oscar nudged Om awake.

Om stirred, looking around and seeing that it was still dark.

"Om, I need to talk to you," Oscar said.

"What is it?"

"The daughters came again."

Om said nothing. He sat up, alert, but stayed calm; ready to listen, ready to learn.

Oscar stood. Began pacing. Trying to calm his racing thoughts.

"I need to ask you something," Oscar said.

Om walked out of the room and into the centre of the temple, finding a step to sit on. Oscar followed, but did not sit. He continued pacing back and forth.

"So you have decided," Om said, "that you know the solution."

"I need to ask, first, I need to know… what do you believe about the afterlife?"

"The afterlife?"

"Yes. Please tell me."

Om took a moment to gather his thoughts. Oscar waited patiently, knowing that Om wished to provide the best answer possible, and knowing that it was crucial that he receive such an answer.

"One enters Parinirvana once dead."

"Parinirvana?"

"Nirvana is a state at which you feel no suffering, where you have let go and are released from karma. Parinirvana is what you enter once dead, where nirvana is waiting for you."

"How? How do you get there?"

"In the sensory world, you are still attached to Mara's troops; to his forces of hatred and delusion. You cannot defeat Mara while you are still attached. You must conquer these attachments first."

"That is it. That is what I thought."

Oscar stopped for a moment, his thoughts racing, then paced again. Suddenly his path was becoming so clear. Suddenly, he understood.

"I learnt a few weeks ago that, to win this war, I would have to defeat The Devil in Hell," Oscar said. "But Hell is not necessarily physical, it is a belief; it is what's inside of us."

Om smiled; Oscar was finally close to understanding. "Go on."

"But I still went to a physical, existential place, and... well, I lost. Which made me think, if that was the only way, I would have lost whether April showed up or not."

"And why is that?"

"Because I still had too much of The Devil in me."

Oscar unknowingly lowered himself to his knees.

"You spoke of me letting go of all that I'm attached to," he said. "That I could not pass through Hell, just as I could not defeat The Devil, with all of this still inside of me."

"Keep going."

"All the time, Om, all the time I'm just so... so angry. So

furious. I feel rage and sometimes I know why, sometimes I don't. I snap at Thea, I snap at Henry, I sit and watch April suffer, and it's all just fuelling it, this torment. Which is why I know I need to face this torment, both literally and figuratively. Only, I need to ask — where could I fight this? I know I need to fight my attachments; I just don't understand where, or how."

"Think about your memories. Think about what you have lost, and what you hold on to, and tell me — what would *your* Parinirvana look like?"

"Man, it would be… April, happy, hugging me. Julian helping me. Derek still alive. My parents proud. All of it."

"And if you were offered that now, would you be able to say no?"

Oscar considered this. He wanted to be honest, but he also knew he had to let the image go.

He stood.

"I think I get it now," he decided. "I spent half an hour in Hell as I didn't want to lose my life. I left because I didn't want to lose April. And, whilst in Hell, I didn't face any true torment. I didn't have to give anything up. There wasn't really any challenge at all."

"So what do you need to do?"

"I have to face those things, however Hell presents them to me. I have to confront all of those things I am attached to, that make me angry, I have to let go of them, and I—"

He closed his eyes, wishing he didn't have to admit what he was about to admit.

"I will have to let go of my life, too."

Om stood. Placed a hand on Oscar's shoulder.

"I can't believe this, Om," Oscar said. "I can't believe what I am about to do."

"Let go of it. There is no suffering when you're losing nothing."

Oscar nodded.

Wiped his tears away.

And decided, more for his own sake, to finally say it aloud.

"I will have to return to Hell to face it again," he said. "To face everything that has tormented me before."

He looked into Om's eyes, knowing there was more, and willing himself to say it.

Finally, he did.

"And to do that," he concluded. "I will have to actually, truly, properly do it."

He composed himself. Stood tall. Stood strong.

He was ready.

He'd say it, and then he was ready.

"I will have to die."

THEN

SIX YEARS OLD

25

THE READING AREA WAS IN THE CLASSROOM'S CORNER. This was not an area as popular as the toy area, or the phonics area, or even the washing hands area. Not that reading wasn't enjoyable — it was because they spent most of their time in this area reading to the teaching assistant.

Oscar hated it. He was a strong reader — that wasn't the problem. For a six-year-old, he could read books meant for much above his age. His favourite was *The Witches* by Roald Dahl — he enjoyed doing the voices for the different characters.

This afternoon, he had a go at another Roald Dahl book his teacher had suggested. It was called *Danny the Champion of the World* and, even though it seemed strange, he was enjoying it.

He was just getting to the bit where they prepared the raisins for the pheasants and, as he turned the page, he glanced upwards.

There he was, across the classroom. Bertrand.

He should have been doing his handwriting exercises like

everyone else, but he wasn't. His pen was still and his exercise book untouched. He just stared.

Bertrand had been away for a few months. Oscar had enjoyed it. It had been a relief from the torment; a welcome break where he had actually enjoyed school. He had no idea where Bertrand had gone, and honestly; he didn't care.

Even the teachers had commented on Oscar's remarkable surge in confidence.

But he was back.

Oscar hadn't seen him at all that day. In fact, he was sure that Bertrand's seat had remained empty during registration, and first lesson.

Yet, here he was now, glaring at Oscar. In one look, he destroyed all the progress Oscar had made. All those conversations Oscar was having with other children, all those friends he'd made, and the breaktimes he played tag instead of sitting in the playground's corner hoping to be left alone. It was for nothing.

Because he was there, across the classroom, watching. His podgy cheeks and scruffy hair and ill-fitting clothes just as they were.

"Come on, Oscar, keep going," the teaching assistant urged.

But Oscar didn't feel like reading.

In fact, he didn't feel like talking at all anymore. He wanted to close his mouth, crawl up into a ball, and never be disturbed again.

"Oscar, you're doing really well, come on."

Bertrand was still glaring. So intently. His determined gaze fixed upon Oscar.

Oscar's lip quivered. His arms shook.

Why couldn't Bertrand leave him alone?

Why did he have to come back?

He could have stayed wherever he was, and Oscar would

have happily read his book. He would get some kind of reward for the amount of reading he'd done; his teacher had promised.

Oscar assumed that wouldn't be happening now.

"Oscar, what's the matter?"

Oscar felt something he couldn't explain. In his belly. A churning, like a grinding, a twisting of his insides like they were wrapping around one another.

The book he held grew warmer, yet he couldn't let it go. His hands would not release it.

"Oscar?"

The pages grew hotter and hotter, his fingertips hurting, and he moaned, cried, unable to explain what was happening.

"Oscar, what is the matter?"

The pages.

They were too hot.

It was too much.

It hurt.

It really hurt.

"Oscar, what–"

Before the teaching assistant could finish her sentence, she had leapt up and out of the way as the book set on fire.

From the open pages, flames danced into the air.

Oscar knew Bertrand had done it, and he knew Bertrand was grinning. But he didn't look up.

He stared at the flames.

"Oscar, put it down!"

The class was screaming now. Everyone was rushing outside.

Oscar didn't look up. They were all just blurs in the corner of his vision.

His gaze was fixed on this book, on the fire, on the sudden combustion warming his skin.

The book was grabbed from his hands and taken away. Oscar lifted his head slightly to see the teacher rushing the book to the sink. She dropped it into the bowl and poured water. The flames died down.

Oscar looked to see if Bertrand was still in his seat.

Just like everyone else, he had left.

Only, unlike everyone else in his class, Bertrand did not return after lunch.

NOW

26

OSCAR SAT ON A STEP AT THE EDGE OF THE TEMPLE.

What had seemed such an ominous, run-down building now seemed to have a renewed sense of beauty. Despite the moss and weeds and crumbling rock, it was an architectural triumph, once a home to many men like Om.

Footsteps tapped lightly on the stone behind him.

"Do you have it?" Oscar asked.

"Yes," Om answered, and sat on the step beside Oscar, holding out a shrub with a green stem and yellow petals.

Oscar didn't take it yet. He took another deep breath and let it go, trying not to question his decision.

"Once it's worked, you must contact Father Lorenzo Romano for me."

"He will come, don't worry."

"Make sure he warns Thea and Henry — once I have left this world, the balance will shift again, and The Devil will have far more power. Restraints will no longer hold him."

Oscar wished he could warn his friends of their enemy's forthcoming surge in power, but he neither had a working phone or the strength to explain to them what he was about to do.

He looked over the forest and admired the view stretching out before him.

"It's funny," he observed. "You only admire the beauty of the world when facing imminent death. I came here and trudged up the steps, thinking this was a shitty temple. And now..."

He looked at the shrub once again.

"Lorenzo will need to take me back to England," he said. "If this works, and that's a big *if,* I will need my body to be there. I mean, I don't know if that will be much use, I don't even know how I'd get back from Hell, especially if I'm dead. I imagine if demons can possess a body then I can too, I just–"

He stopped talking. He was rambling. Wasting time. Delaying the inevitable.

He could not afford to waste time.

He took the shrub from Om and held it between his fingers.

Oscar went to ask — *so will I go back to purgatory, like last time?* But he knew his answer. He was about to take his own life, which was a sin — he would be going straight to Hell.

He gulped. Tried to divert his thoughts to other things.

Anything but the conclusive nature of death.

"So what's it called?" Oscar asked.

"Aconitum Coreanum. It is also known as Korean monkshood."

"And how long does it take?"

"Your average dose might take two to six hours. This dose, however, should be almost instant. Maybe a few minutes of suffering first."

"Of suffering?"

"Vomiting, nausea, that kind of thing."

"So I might die in a puddle of my own sick?"

"Possibly, possibly not."

"I just — I don't know…"

Again, Oscar tried to push his concerns away, tried to stop thinking about it — but dying was not something one can run from.

"How does it actually kill me?"

"Paralysis of the heart."

He gulped and wished he hadn't asked.

He stood. A sudden, decisive motion. He just needed to do this.

"Are you sure this is a good idea?" Oscar asked.

"I think you should do what you believe–"

"No, give me a proper answer. Is this a good idea?"

Om smiled. Stood. Put a hand on Oscar's shoulder.

"You are strong," Om said. "You are ready."

Oscar nodded.

Stared at the contents of his hand.

Strange how eating something that looked so harmless, just a simple plant, could have such devastating consequences.

He closed his eyes.

Lifted his hand to his open mouth.

Paused. Tried not to consider the stupidity of killing himself, what could go wrong, how he could end up not being there for April's final days, the mess he had left for Thea, how he would never get to tell his parents he wasn't actually a failure — he ignored the rage burning inside of him, the resentment that it was always him who had to do this; the fury that, once again, he was returning to the place no human ever wished to go.

He could die forever, never come back, and end up stuck in Hell.

He wanted to cry and scream and hear it echo back at

him. He wanted to lash out and tell Om he could go. Oscar did not want to die; he was too young.

He wished he did not have to be the one to endure these horrific tasks.

But he was. And he had to accept that.

Fuck it.

Without allowing himself to think about it anymore, he shoved the poison into his mouth and swallowed.

He opened his eyes. Looked at Om.

Felt nothing, at first.

Then it hit him. The clenching of his insides. The tingle of his limbs.

Vomit lurched through his throat and took him to his knees with the power of its hurl. He spewed lumpy bile over the ground, then was sick again.

He tried to walk away from the sick, not wanting to die in the puddle, and made a few steps before he fell to his side.

His mouth burned. His face tingled. His nose, his ears, they went numb. His abdomen felt on fire.

He closed his eyes, waited for it to pass, but it felt too bad. It was awful. He was having to die in pain and there was nothing he could do but accept it and wait.

His limbs tingled and he could no longer lift his arms. He kicked his leg, if only to show that he could, then he lost the ability.

He lay still on the floor, spread out, staring at the clear, blue sky. His forehead perspired, and sweat trickled into this eye. He tried to breathe, but he no longer could.

Then came the pain in his arm, and in his chest.

His heart was failing.

He closed his eyes and waited for death.

He didn't have to wait long.

27

In just a few minutes, the faces around the house turned from a few to many. The sparse bodies hidden in the shadows had become a mass of empty figures, waiting, dormant.

"Why are they just standing there?" asked Henry.

Thea joined him at the living room window.

"What would you rather they do?" Thea asked. "Try to get into the house?"

A storm raged outside the window. Wind fought the rain, pellets of water bombarded the grass, and puddles accumulated.

It was like the weather was at war with itself.

"I don't want them to attack, but I don't understand why they aren't."

"Last time they tried, we beat them."

"But things are different now. We didn't have their leader tied to a bed."

A bump shook the ceiling.

It sounded like two heavy feet stepping on the floor.

Thea stared upwards. They'd heard a lot of noises. Hopefully, this was just another one of them.

"They aren't here to kill us," she said absently, her focus on the ceiling. "They are here to worship."

A few more pounds came from above, like footsteps. Slow, weighty steps.

"They are here to meet their leader."

Bump.

Bump.

Bump.

Creak.

"What was that?" whispered Henry.

Thea's wide eyes met Henry's. She didn't answer.

Bump.

Bump.

They grew louder.

Like they were out of the room.

Thea edged to the door, unwillingly forcing her feet to inch forward.

Henry did not move.

He watched her, staying at the window.

Thea peered forward, so she could just about see the top step.

Bump.

Bump.

Pause.

Bump.

Bump.

Pause.

Each step was heavy, like falling then regaining balance. A quick stumble and stop.

And each step was becoming louder.

Bump.

Bump.

A shadow appeared over the top step. It was already dark, the soundtrack of a blizzard matching the flickers of darkness from the upstairs window.

Bump.

Bump.

Two legs appeared at the top of the steps. Bare, unshaven ankles. Flaking dead skin. Ripped pyjamas unveiling the scorned flesh.

A foot met the next step, then the other foot met the next, the movement disjointed; robotically chaotic.

As if whoever was walking down the stairs had never used those legs.

Like a creature getting used to its body

Another bump, and another, followed by a succession, and it met the bottom step.

"April…"

The name passed her lips without intention or meaning.

April stood before them, but at the same time, she didn't.

Crotch soaked with crusty blood. Hair greasy with dried sweat. Face pale and skin cracked. Lips dry. Body stiff. Grin bigger than the face could handle.

"Henry…" she whispered. "The crucifix…"

"What?" he blurted out, loud and with no tact.

Thea clenched her fist and willed herself to remain calm, not removing her eyes from the approaching body.

"The crucifix," she snapped, a little louder.

"The crucifix?"

"Yes!"

Henry rushed to the crucifix hanging on the wall but, before he grabbed it, he stopped. Saw her. And panicked.

"Oh my God…"

"Hurry, Henry!"

Henry stole the crucifix from the wall and rushed forward to Thea.

The edge of the cross had just met her fingers when it happened.

Lightning struck outside, coinciding with the lifting of April's arm. Thea soared across the room, into Henry, and into the wall.

Using April's body as a helpless vessel, it moved forward, its breath croaking, its face full of cockiness, full of victory.

"Thea," it said, its voice low-pitched and booming. "You should have left when Oscar did."

28

OM KNELT AT OSCAR'S SIDE.

No one wishes to provide the means for someone to die. Especially not Om.

But there was no choice.

He could not see him, but he could already feel Lorenzo walking up the steps. He had not contacted Lorenzo, but Lorenzo would know when the shift in balance occurred, and he would know it was time to collect the body.

For Om, death was normally a cheerful occasion, not a sad one. It would give the deceased an opportunity to enter a new life or enter Parinirvana.

Only now, the boy was entering Hell.

He placed a hand on the boy's shoulder, closed his eyes, and bowed his head.

"Om ami deva hrih," he chanted, quietly, so only he and the wind could hear it. "Om ami deva hrih, om ami deva hrih."

He did this until Lorenzo reached the top step, and he had to stop.

"Well?" Lorenzo prompted, his lip upturned, his voice impatient. "Is he dead?"

"I thought you said you'd know when he is dead."

"You don't ever just give a straight answer, do you?"

Lorenzo stepped forward and looked over the corpse.

"I hope this works," Lorenzo said.

"And if it doesn't?"

Lorenzo sneered at Om.

"Then we are all damned to Hell."

Lorenzo took out a radio and turned around. He had a mumbled conversation that didn't last long, then turned back to the body.

"The helicopter will be here soon," he said.

Om did not ask why Lorenzo hadn't just arrived in the helicopter. Maybe Lorenzo had been nearby, waiting impatiently for the death of his warrior.

He seemed annoyed that he'd had to wait so long for Oscar to die.

"What?" Lorenzo directed at Om, and Om realised he was staring. "You think the way I'm acting is callous?"

"You act as you wish."

Lorenzo snorted a laugh, grinning sarcastically.

The sound of a helicopter grew in the distance.

"Are you going to help me move the body?" Lorenzo asked.

"I will not move this body."

"Too weak?"

"The body must be cold before it is touched or moved. The soul doesn't leave the body just because the body has stopped breathing. It takes longer."

"He is dead!" Lorenzo declared. "His soul is in Hell now, far away from his body."

The helicopter approached. Lorenzo stood and waved his arms.

Om watched as Lorenzo beckoned the helicopter closer, and it landed. They strapped Oscar's body to a transportable gurney with little care, wheeled him onto the helicopter, and fixed the gurney in place.

Om watched. He had done his part now, or so it seemed. But a feeling told him he still had one more move to make.

After all, he was old, and this may be the last chance he had to face the opponent he had fought so many years ago.

Just as they were about to leave, he stepped forward.

"I am coming with you," he said.

Lorenzo frowned. "Are you kidding?"

"I wish to come."

"I thought you couldn't leave this temple?"

"I can leave, I just do so with the risk of Mara finding me."

"Mara? You mean The Devil?"

"I am ready to meet him again. I am ready to do my part."

Lorenzo sighed. Looked over his shoulder at the pilot.

They did have an empty seat.

"Fine," he said.

Om walked to the helicopter. After taking a final glance back at his temple, he sat down and fixed the seatbelt across his waist.

He looked at Oscar's body, which appeared deceptively peaceful.

"Is his soul gone now?" Lorenzo asked.

"Oh, it's gone," Om said. "He is on his own now, wherever he is."

29

Oscar's feet met rock, and the heat was immediately familiar.

His feet were barefoot. His clothes were rags. His skin was bloodied and bruised. Hell had chosen this image for him, and he quickly came to accept it.

Lava spewed over the edges of his mound of stone, screams echoed in the distance, and demons flew above the scorched sky.

He knew where he was.

He had been here before.

He wasn't immune to the torment, but he was prepared for it. One could never get used to such conditions; to be in Hell was to be in permanent pain. Every muscle felt weak, every limb felt like a burden, and every movement was a struggle.

He moved his leg forward, and it felt like wading through water.

He considered shouting for The Devil to come and face him but quickly remembered:

The Devil is not here.

He stood strong. Straightened his back, despite how much it throbbed.

"Well?" he shouted, his voice reverberating back to him. "Is no one coming to collect me?"

A roar was his answer.

A figure emerged from the grey clouds, large and ominous. It appeared to have three heads. It was riding something.

Oscar braced himself, and tried not to be afraid.

As it grew closer, he could finally see what this beast looked like. Three heads: one of a human, one of a bull, one of a ram. Tail of a serpent. Eyes full of flames. Riding a bear.

This was Balam. Prince of Hell.

So this was who The Devil must have left in charge.

Balam paused, hovering over Oscar, casting his fiery gaze over the insolent fool who dared enter the underworld for a second time.

"Do you know why I am here?" Oscar asked.

Balam did not respond.

Oscar stepped forward.

"I'm ready," he said, his voice determined. "Whatever you have for me, whatever you will put me through — bring it on."

Balam lifted his chin, leered, then grinned.

He nodded with a slight bow as if to say, *as you wish.*

He soared away into the distance, leaving Oscar alone.

Before Oscar could question why he'd left, the faint patter of a child's feet approached him from behind.

The messenger.

He wondered what form it would take. April? Julian? Thea?

But, as he turned around, he could not have expected to see the face he saw.

At first, he didn't recognise the young girl. He knew that

he knew her, but he couldn't figure out where from. He thought and thought, searching his memory for her face.

Then, in a moment of grave realisation, he knew who she was.

And he knew that the torment was just beginning.

"Hello," he said. "Have you come to take me somewhere?"

She nodded, a face of delight at the prospect of leading him to his doom.

"You didn't save me, you know," she said.

"What?"

"You didn't, I just think you need to know that."

"You aren't really her."

She frowned. "Yes, I am. What, you think I'm just some figment of your imagination?"

"I think you're a figment of Hell."

"No, it's me. Really. Even after you exorcised Ardat Lili from my body, I just kept reliving what had happened. You created a life I couldn't bear to live. I was barely a teenager before I took my life."

"Just take me wherever you are taking me."

"How many others do you think did the same?"

"Just hurry."

"How many girls and boys did you save, only to condemn them to trauma and death?"

"This isn't working."

"You think I'm the only one? You caused this."

"No, I didn't."

"Yes, you did. I needed psychiatric help, and you put me through an ancient, outdated ritual."

"Stop it."

"You haven't even checked up on how any of us are doing, have you? No aftercare. No afterthought. We were a job, and you moved on."

"I saved you, dammit! I *saved* you!"

Kaylee Kemple fell silent. She smiled, satisfied that she had finally found the reaction she wanted. This would evidently be easier than she'd thought.

Oscar scalded himself. He was better than that.

He *had* to be better than that.

"Shall we?" she asked, and turned, ready to take him to his first torment.

He followed and, almost immediately, she had disappeared, and the cells of a prison surrounded him.

THEA FELT THE BACK OF HER HEAD. ITS COLLISION WITH THE fireplace had caused it to bleed, but there wasn't that much blood. She'd be fine.

She looked up, groggy, waiting for her vision to readjust.

The crucifix lay on the floor next to her. Henry was to her left, cowering against the wall.

Above her and across the room, it stood in the hallway. Stretching its arms. Looking at its hands, its body, its legs; not so much admiring as coming to terms with it. For something so powerful, a mortal body must be like a prison cell, and Thea knew The Devil would look to release himself from it as soon as possible.

She could not let that happen.

It turned April's body toward the hallway mirror. It stepped closer, fogging its reflection with her breath. He fish-hooked her cheek, lifting it up, exposing the gums that held her teeth in place.

He mushed her face together, squishing the nose then spreading it, watching the wrinkles on her forehead curl up then spread out.

It looked down at her body. Felt for its arms, dug dirty nails into her flesh, grabbed her breasts as if he was trying to pull them off.

His face turned, angry. Like he was undignified to be in a young woman's body. That this humiliation was making him furious, and somebody needed to suffer as a result.

He turned its sneer toward Thea, his grimace contorting April's features into a visage of wrath that she could never have produced.

Thea did not wait.

She grabbed the crucifix, stood, held it toward him, and edged forward as she shouted her prayer, speaking quickly and clearly.

"That you spare us, that you pardon us, that you bring us true penance."

It lifted April's arm, clenching her fist. Thea was lifted from the ground and smacked into the wall.

She hit her head and fell, dizzily. She ignored the concussion. She refused unconsciousness.

She had promised Oscar.

She was stronger than this.

She saw Henry quivering in the corner.

"Help me!" she said.

Henry shook his head.

"Help me, or what is the point of you being here?"

He seemed to accept this and hesitantly stepped forward, each step as wary as the last.

She turned back to The Devil.

"That you govern and preserve your Holy Church, that you preserve our Holy Father."

April's mouth opened, her jaw broken, and her chin fell to the base of her neck. Through that mouth came an almighty roar; the screams of the damned, with every ounce of suffering and pain caught in multiple shrieks.

"Give me the answer, Henry," she instructed. "Lord, have mercy."

"Lord, have mercy," Henry answered from behind her.

"Christ, have mercy."

"Christ, have mercy."

She pushed herself forward, but with its scream came a destructive gust of wind, catching everything in its path. The door to the living room battered against its hinges, the sofa shifted, the light above swinging back and forth.

"Christ, hear us!" Thea persisted, shouting to be heard.

"Christ, graciously hear us."

Thea knew this wouldn't work. She knew that the rites of exorcism would not end this attack, nor would it stop their enemy from leaving the house and bringing destruction to the world.

These prayers were for protection. The more they fought, the less that could be done to them.

They would figure out what to do once it left; for now, they had to stay alive.

They could do nothing to stop it if they were dead.

"God, the Father in Heaven!"

"Have mercy on us!"

"Holy Trinity, one God!"

"Have mercy on us!"

It wasn't enough. Another scream accompanied another thrust of the arms, and Thea and Henry flew across the room

This was only the beginning.

This was The Devil just beginning to find its power and discover its abilities; it was the equivalent of a toddler learning to walk.

Thea continued to pray but, inwardly, she prayed that Oscar would just walk through that door with the answers. That he would come in, saying he had it solved, and he knew what to do.

No such event occurred.

The scream ended.

The creature inhabiting such a fragile set of skin and bone edged into the living room.

Thea feared for her life. She feared for Henry's. She needed to fight harder than she ever had before. Even though she was on the floor, even though she was hurt, and even though she was vastly overpowered — she had to do whatever she could to resist.

"Holy Mary, pray for us," she said, her voice coming out in a hoarse whisper.

"Pray for us," she heard Henry say from behind her.

It approached. The once welcoming shadow of April's posture changed to a heavy hunch.

It reached April's hand toward her.

Thea clutched the crucifix. Threw her arms upwards, directed it at him, projected all of her energy into the resolve with which she held it.

"For haughty men have risen up against me, and fierce men seek my life," Thea said.

April's hand wavered, but it reached it out again.

"Turn back the evil upon my foes, *in your faithfulness destroy them!*"

Her arms shook and her voice broke but, even from her position on the floor, she did not give in.

It paused. Looked down on her like it was taking pity.

"This won't stop me forever, you know," it said. "Soon it will all be over, and I will not grant you the sweet release of death. I will keep you as my slave, and you will suffer forever."

"Oscar will stop you. I know he will."

It cackled.

"Oscar is exactly where I want him."

It turned, walk out of the house, and the room fell silent.
Henry crawled to her side like he thought it was over.
But the end was only just beginning.

OSCAR STOOD ALONE IN THE PRISON.

It wasn't just any prison.

It was Gloucester Prison.

Well, it was Gloucester Prison as it had once been presented to them. Actually, this prison had been taken over by an evil presence that had stopped Derek and the Sensitives from knowing what was really happening.

They had all thought a sadistic governor and a girl's ghost were the problems. Little had they realised that this place was overrun with manifestations, and the spirit of the demented prison governor had almost hung Derek by the throat until death.

He looked behind him. Kaylee Kemple had gone.

His next torment was about to begin.

Yet, it didn't seem that bad. He had already defeated this prison's entities. He had already overcome it and saved Derek.

It felt strange to be here. Despite how far he'd come, he couldn't help but fall back into the person he was when he battled against the entities within this prison. A timid boy who lacked confidence in himself and in his convictions. He hadn't even had the strength to tell April how he'd felt — and look at him now. He was leading what was left of the Sensitives.

It's odd, isn't it? Never mind how far we have come, it only takes one old, familiar situation to make us feel young and stupid all over again.

He stepped forward, and a small sound caught his attention. It came from a cell a little further along. It sounded like crying.

He approached, peering in.

An ageing man lay on the ground, huddled up in the foetal position. His body was thin and weak. His walking stick was across the cell. He was sobbing pathetically.

"Derek?"

It surprised Oscar to see him like this. Even at the end of his life, Derek had been dignified and strong. He was a wise man, a true leader, and one who always knew the right thing to do.

Not Oscar, nor anyone else, had ever seen him cry like this.

It was unusual, and Oscar remained cautious.

"Oscar," he said, reaching his hand out.

Oscar edged toward him. Moved to his knees. Placed his hand on Derek's forehead.

He was burning.

Oscar shook his head defiantly. He couldn't let himself fall for such obvious trickery.

"This isn't you," Oscar said.

"Oscar, please..."

"No, this isn't you, I know it. You are in Heaven. I've seen it. You've spoken to me."

"*Something* spoke to you. Whatever Heaven needed you to see spoke to you. Don't be such a fool..."

"But why would you be–"

"It's forever. Reliving this moment forever. It's happened so many times I don't know how long I've been here. Again and again he comes, at the same time, with the same–"

The creak of a door opening silenced Derek. His eyes widened.

"I don't believe you," Oscar insisted. "You would never have been sent to Hell. They wouldn't allow it."

"Who are *they*, Oscar? Who do you think cares that much?"

Footsteps.

"It isn't true. You're not in Hell. You–"

"Derek Lansdale," came a booming voice from behind him.

He rotated his head to look, and there he was. The prison governor, Jackson Kullins.

"You're not real," Oscar decided.

"Oscar, don't," Derek whimpered. "Don't make it angry. Don't make it mad."

Oscar stood. This was exactly what he had to contend with. This was what Hell would try to do.

He strode out of the cell and marched toward Kullins.

Oscar put his hand on Kullins' throat and pushed him back, pressing him against the wall.

Derek still moaned for him to stop, telling him not to infuriate Kullins.

Oscar ignored him. It wasn't real.

It couldn't be.

Otherwise every other time he'd seen Derek since his passing was a lie from Heaven. And that would be a torment he couldn't face right now.

So he squeezed his hand around Kullins' throat. Squeezed harder.

Kullins did not struggle.

Flickers of his true form appeared. Claws. Fangs. Dark yellow and red eyes.

Oscar strangled harder and harder still.

A knife appeared in his hand.

Where had that come from?

It didn't matter.

He held the knife back and swung it into the gut of Kullins.

Except it wasn't Kullins anymore.

He wasn't in the prison.

He was in his bathroom at home.

Julian was laying beneath him, a knife in his gut.

The knife Oscar had just swung.

Julian could do nothing but live out the last moment of his life — a moment that had otherwise been unwitnessed.

And he had to do it beneath Oscar, who had just killed him.

HAIL LASHED DOWN LIKE IT WAS ATTACKING THE WORLD; LIKE nature's true aggression had finally been unleashed. The cloud had frozen despite the heat, and the wind had carried sleet to Earth with a ferocity the world rarely witnessed.

The Devil relished it.

He held April's arms out as he walked, lifting the head of his mortal body and feeling the sting on his face.

Behind him, his congregation followed. They had gathered, waiting for him to rise in power, waiting to be guided.

It had all come to fruition.

Millions of years of trying, and finally The Devil had arrived, finding his way into this world, ready to spread his carnage.

As he walked, more followed.

Each of them trapped in their fleshy prisons.

But that wouldn't be for much longer...

He felt the power of Hell grow, coming to him slowly, bit by bit. Soon, he wouldn't need this vessel to survive, and his followers would no longer need theirs. The Devil could break free of it and unleash his true form onto the world.

They would flee.

They would cry.

And they would suffer.

He was cast out of Heaven by a so-called loving god — which, by the way, was not a *loving* thing to do — and had been trapped in the fire ever since; left to rule the flames and evil of the world.

He should have been killed.

He should have been torn apart and stopped an eternity ago.

But Heaven would not do such a thing. They would banish him, but they would be too good to end him.

The pretentious, world-loving bastards.

After he'd dealt with this world, Heaven would be next. He'd find a way to return, and he'd tear all those peaceful souls apart, just like he would with his human slaves.

He neared a hill.

He walked up its steep drop. The legs of his body ached, but he ignored it. He wasn't used to mild pain like this, but it was temporary.

The followers came, walking where he walked, remaining behind him.

He rose to the top of the hill, and there he stopped. At the highest point. Looking out upon the world, upon the view. So many lights, so many buildings, so many cars.

So many people.

He enjoyed this immensely; watching the world he would soon be his. Watching the people go about their business without any idea what was coming.

The weather continued its onslaught upon them. It commanded authority he would soon assume. It controlled these pathetic morsels and made them rush for shelter.

Soon, there would be no shelter.

Not from him.

He rose April's arms into the sky. All his disciples dropped to a single knee and bowed their heads in his direction. A circle of loyal supporters, ready to worship and do his bidding. He would keep them dormant until he was ready, ensuring they left the Sensitives to him alone to kill.

It was happening.

It was wonderful.

It was glorious.

And, as he closed his eyes and tuned into his senses, he could feel more awakening, more realising where he was.

They were all on their way.

33

ALL OVER THE WORLD, THEY AWOKE.

Some of them had already declared their presence. They had made the host they inhabited suffer. They had pushed the mortal soul out of reach and forced violence upon their victim's families.

Some of them had waited. Remained in the background of their human, dormant, anticipating the right moment.

This was that moment.

He was growing in power. He was calling them.

It was time.

The beginning of the end was upon the world, those that remained would soon succumb to the flames, and humans would no longer be the dominant species of this planet.

Horace, a farmer in Cheshire with a wife and two children, sat at the table, eating his breakfast and reading the newspaper.

He had no idea what lurked within. He'd heard whispers, seen things out of the corner of his eyes, but he had not been one to believe in superstitious nonsense.

Now, Horace was pushed to the background.

The demon within dropped the newspaper, picked up the fork, and looked to the wife, daughter and son eating their bacon sandwiches beside him.

He stood. Raised the fork and stared at Horace's wife.

"What are you doing?" she asked, startled. She had never seen this look on his face before.

He plunged the fork downwards, lodging it deep into the side of her throat, and retracting it just as quickly.

Before the children could scream, he'd picked the son up by the hair and dug the fork into his belly, not once, but again and again and again and again.

The daughter tried to run, but he grabbed her before she managed to get away.

He stuck the fork into her neck and left it there.

He walked onward, heeding the call, knowing he wouldn't need this body much longer.

Marion's demon had not remained hidden. In her home in Calais, they had shackled her to chains in the basement while her family beseeched the local priest to help. They hadn't slept, what with the screaming and the moaning and the screeching — all of which came from Marion, not the demon. The demon was playing with her insides, was rolling around her body, violating whichever organ it found, prompting Marion to shout out in pain.

By the time The Devil had summoned his disciples, amalgamation incarnation had long since occurred. The demon had remained in chains to toy with the family; to make them believe they were safe, that they could help the wench this demon had infected.

But, as they stood before her, the priest beginning his prayers, the demon within felt the power of its leader grow.

It pulled one arm forward and took the chain out of the wall, then pulled the other and did the same.

It swung the chains into the priest's cranium. He collapsed, and the demon continued swinging the chains into the priest's skull until it was completely smashed.

"Marion?" the husband whimpered, wanting to run for safety, but resisting the impulse. He would not leave the woman he loved, so he tried to pull her off the priest.

Fool.

The demon stood tall and swung the chains until they were wrapped thrice around the husband's throat, then pulled.

The demon looked into the man's eyes as he choked, wanting him to see Marion's eyes as he died.

Once his last breath ended, the demon stood, and walked in the direction for which he was being called, through the channel tunnel and into the British Isles.

Chet, a pilot flying a private plane over the North Sea, on route from Denmark to Canada, felt it happen.

As soon as the plane was passing over England, he directed it downwards.

His co-pilot objected. Chet beat him to death with the fire extinguisher.

The screams grew into a crescendo as the plane headed downwards. He took the parachute and leapt out of the cabin.

He floated gently to the ground as a momentous flame grew from this terrible, most unfortunate incident. So much screaming then, suddenly, nothing.

Chet, or rather, the demon inside of Chet, landed on a field nearby.

He disconnected the parachute and walked.

All over the world, demons grew in strength. They awoke, discarded their restraints, and dispatched of their victim's families. They walked out of their homes and directed themselves to where their leader was waiting for them.

Each of them waiting for the moment they could hardly believe was finally here.

34

OSCAR'S EYES AND JULIAN'S EYES WERE FIXED, INCHES AWAY from each other, like a trance had kept them together.

Oscar's were full of fear, consumed with terror at what he'd done.

Julian's were full of pain, gripped by agony; stuck in the moment of death as if it had been prolonged; like he was in slow-motion.

Oscar hated it. He didn't want to watch this. He wanted to look away.

Yet, somehow, he couldn't. It was like something was making him look, like two hands had gripped his cheeks and held his head in place.

Julian fell so slowly you could barely tell he was falling, his face slowly melding into various contortions of suffering.

Blood trickled like a river between Oscar's fingers.

In a sudden change of speed, Julian landed on the floor of the bathroom and screamed, then did not stop screaming. His moans of anguish, his hollers of desperation — they just continued. The torture of dying vocalised in such a way that Oscar wished he did not have to listen.

"You did this!"

Oscar covered his ears.

"You did this! You did it!"

He could not block out the sound.

"You killed me, you rat-bastard, you killed me!"

Oscar paused. He remained in his state of despair, but something was gradually moving him out of it.

It was something Julian had just called him.

Rat-bastard.

It sounded so… wrong.

It didn't fit with Julian's voice.

It wasn't a term Julian had ever called Oscar, and Oscar couldn't imagine Julian calling anyone else it. Julian saved many profanities for Oscar, but this was not one of them.

"It's not you," Oscar whispered.

He felt stupid for only just realising it.

He had been in a prison then in his bathroom so quickly, yet he had accepted that as reality. He had accepted Derek's suffering, had accepted that he had directly killed Julian, and he had accepted that it was all happening in front of him, slowly and tediously to draw out the suffering.

But it wasn't happening. It was all a lie.

Yet, below him, Julian did not stop wriggling.

Or, should he say, the *thing* masquerading as Julian; the *image* of him did not stop wriggling.

He writhed and moaned and suffered. He died in pain, just as he had done in life, and even though Oscar knew it wasn't real, he hated seeing it.

Whether this was a performance for his benefit or not, this may well have been what it was like for Julian as he died.

Then he realised — Julian did not die from stabbing himself in the belly. He'd slit his own throat.

As if reacting to Oscar's thought — to the point at which Oscar wondered whether his thoughts were still private —

Julian took the knife from his stomach and placed it in the side of the throat.

"No," he said. "Don't make me do it. Please."

He dragged the knife across his skin.

"Please…"

He pulled the blade across his flesh until it met the other side of his throat. Blood sprayed like a water fountain, a squirt of thick red covering the tiles of the bathroom.

When April discovered him the next day, the walls had been covered. The blood had dried up, but it was everywhere.

Oscar was still watching.

Why was he still watching?

Because it still hurts.

He and Julian had had a mixed relationship. But, despite the forthright nature of Julian's conversations, he was there for him. He never left. He took care of April, and without acknowledging it, he took care of Oscar too.

Oscar had not thought of that. Even at Julian's funeral, he was concentrating on taking care of April, making sure she was okay. He had never really thought it to himself — *Julian is dead.*

Not just dead.

Killed, most likely by demonic influence.

And whilst Oscar had not actually held the knife in real life, he had created this mess. Many had died as a result. Had he made different choices, Julian would still be alive. April would not have suffered losing the closest thing she had to a brother, or even a father.

And here, watching Julian suffer the last moments of his life in front of him, he had no choice but to acknowledge it.

He had no choice but to watch it.

To watch what Julian may have gone through; the pain with which his life would have ended.

And, as Oscar watched, he allowed himself to feel what he had previously fought away. All the regret, the hurt, and the repressed, conflicting feelings — they were unleashed, flooding his body with remorse and regret and a thousand other emotions he did not understand nor care to appreciate.

He felt it.

He allowed it.

Then it stopped.

In one decision, made swiftly and decisively, he stopped feeling it.

He looked at Julian's body, now laying before him as a corpse, and he accepted it.

He let it go.

Just as Om had said, attaching himself to his pain would only serve Hell more.

So he relieved himself of the burden, despite feeling so undeserving of such liberties.

He crouched. Put a hand on the image of Julian, on his bloody shoulder.

"I'm sorry," he said.

He stood, and it was done.

That part of his life was over, and he was finished with it.

He opened the door to the bathroom, ready to walk out.

And, as he did, he heard a baby crying.

He bowed his head, knowing what he was about to face. While had just escaped from his first torment, his torture was only just beginning.

THEN

TEN YEARS OLD

35

It was a sunny Saturday afternoon, and Oscar's parents had granted him permission to ride his bike around the estate.

He did this alone, like he did most things alone. Not that he minded his solitude; in fact, he quite liked it. He only felt sad about it because people called him things. Things like *loner*. The other day a group of boys sang *All By Yourself* at him, and he couldn't understand why it mattered whether he was alone.

But, on this particularly sunny day, he had looked forward to an afternoon by himself. Even though his parents had said he could only cycle around the estate, he had gone a little further, to a field beside his school.

The school always looked so strange on a Saturday. None of the lights were on. No one was in. The gate was chained. He kind of liked it.

Once in the field, he cycled to his favourite tree. It was a willow tree. Its branches reminded him of the haircut a boy at school had; floppy and messy. Still, the branches were large and drooped over him, which meant they could conceal him in his own world while he lay under it.

He left his bike by the side of the tree, then leant against the trunk. From his bag, he took out his book and his comic. He had *I Am Legend* to read — a book about vampires. The main character in the book, Robert Neville, was the last man alive on earth, and no one teased him about being alone. Oscar was two chapters in, and he was enjoying it.

He also had a *Beano* comic. His mum said he was getting too old for them, but he still liked it, and she still bought them for him occasionally.

He decided he'd continue with the book. He'd enjoyed the beginning and was eager to find out what happened.

He was only a few pages in when it sounded like someone was calling his name.

"Oscar."

He looked up.

No one was there. At least, he couldn't see anyone from between the branches. He was fairly well hidden and, if someone could see him, they surely couldn't tell who he was.

It was probably just the wind.

Even though there was only a gentle breeze, sometimes it sounds louder when pushing between the leaves.

He continued reading.

"Oscar."

It was still only a whisper, but was a little louder than the last time, and definitely sounded like someone was speaking.

He ignored it.

He persisted with reading, only half taking in the words on the page.

A few minutes went by and he heard nothing else. Deciding that it was just in his head, he became more and more engrossed in his book — meaning that, when his name was spoken again, and with more gusto, it really made him jump.

"Oscar!"

He leapt to his knees.

It was a boy's voice.

He recognised the voice.

He dreaded that voice.

He looked around, trying to see if he was here, trying to see if it was him.

It couldn't be. He was alone; he was sure of it.

Yet, in the distance, beyond the gaps of the branches, there was something.

There was *someone*.

About his height. Not moving. Just standing still.

He placed his bookmark in his book and put the book in his bag.

He edged forward, keeping this figure in his eyeline, not looking away.

As he made it closer to the overhanging branches, he could tell a bit more about this figure.

He was chubby.

Familiar.

With his arms shaking, Oscar made it to the edge of the branches, and he could just about see…

Bertrand.

But the branches still blocked his view. He had to be sure — he had to be absolutely positive.

He quickly brushed the branches aside to reveal whoever was stood there.

But no one stood there.

No boy. No figure. Nothing.

Just a field.

Even though he was still alone, he felt frightened. He was sure he'd seen him; he was so, so sure.

He wasn't taking any chances.

He rushed back to his bike, leapt upon the seat, and cycled away — riding quickly past the point at which he thought the boy had stood.

He did not stop until he reached home.

NOW

THE TORRENTIAL HAIL HAMMERED AGAINST THE OUTSIDE OF the windows, but the inside of the house was quiet. Thea and Henry lay unconscious.

The evil that had overcome the house had left. The noises had stopped. The stink had gone. It was empty.

This was the first thing Thea acknowledged when she came around. The absence of what had been. The feeling of liberation, that the house was now free, and that they were alone.

But it wasn't good news. Even though the house was now safe, the rest of the world was not.

She looked around. Readjusted. Took in the room.

She was in the living room.

How had she fallen unconscious? She didn't remember doing so. Her last memory was of laying on the floor, but defiantly, telling The Devil that Oscar would stop him.

She had no idea where he had taken April's body, what he was doing, and how long this world had left.

This was the end; there was no doubt about it.

Oscar had told them to keep April's body in the house, to stop The Devil from getting out.

They had failed.

"Henry?" Thea said, weakly, propping herself up on her elbows and peering at the still body across the room.

The crucifix lay beside her hand.

"Henry, wake up," she urged.

She pushed herself to her knees, paused, and held herself up by her shaking arms.

"Henry, come on."

Henry's body moved a little. He groaned.

Thea crawled across the carpet to his side. She knelt over him, pushing his body, tapping his cheek.

"Come on," she persisted.

His head turned.

"Henry…"

His eyelids fluttered and lifted. He looked confused.

"Henry, we have to go. We have to find April."

"What — what's going on?"

He looked around, reminding himself of where he was and what had happened.

Thea helped him sit up. He rubbed his eyes, and she watched his face change as the memory returned.

"We let her go," Henry said, his voice small. "He escaped."

"That's right. That's why we have to go find her."

"But how will we–"

"I don't know, but we will, and that is why you have to get up."

She pushed herself to her feet, hoping that if she found more energy, so would he. She paused to let a head rush pass, then began gathering supplies.

The crucifix. Holy water. Rosary beads.

The items she would take into battle, just as Oscar had taught her.

Except, this was no ordinary exorcism, and she did not know what she was about to march them both into.

They could stay at home. They could remain in safety and watch the world end from the sofa. They could die peacefully, unlike so many others who would not be so fortunate.

But she couldn't. Despite the odds against them, the Sensitives were the last defence, and they had to keep battling to their last breath.

They could not afford themselves the luxury of admitting they had lost.

By the time Thea had gathered what she needed and returned to the living room, Henry was sitting on the sofa, massaging his temples.

"We need to go," she said.

Henry didn't look up. He buried his head in his hands.

"We don't have time for this," she insisted.

He kept his face hidden and shook his head.

"Henry, come on."

"I can't, I can't, I can't…"

Thea shifted her weight from one foot to the other, very much aware that time was against them. She knelt in front of him and placed her hands on his arms.

"Henry, we need to go."

"I can't… I'm not like you. I only beat that horde of possessed a few weeks ago because you were there. I only survived The Devil coming downstairs because you were there. All I do is hold you back."

He lifted his head. His eyes were red, his cheeks damp.

"I think I'm going to go home," he said. "If the world's going to end, I should be with my family."

"I need you, Henry."

"You don't. You do much better without–"

"Would you stop it!" she snapped.

She tried to calm herself down, then realised she didn't want to calm down. She opened her mouth and unleashed.

"You think I'm not scared? You think I'm not terrified? You think I am not completely and totally out of my depth here?"

"But you're a Sensitive who–"

"Please, I've been here for about a year! The only reason Oscar keeps me around is because of the strength of my skill, not my experience. I have no idea what I'm doing, and I fully expect us to lose this battle."

Henry shook his head despairingly. "Then why bother?"

She placed her hands on his cheeks and ensured he was looking at her.

"Because what else do we do? We aren't allowed to give up. It is up to us, and us alone, to give it one last try."

She took his right hand in her right hand, clasped it, used it to hoist him up.

"Until the end," she said.

He looked back at her, forcing resolve through the dread and the tears.

"Until the end," he echoed.

He took his crucifix and, together, they left the house.

"HI, DADDY," SAID HAYLEY.

Except, it wasn't Hayley, was it?

As Oscar stared at this child in the centre of his living room, months old but already talking and the size of a toddler, he reminded himself of that. She had toys in front of her, Duplo or something, but wasn't playing with them. They spread out across the carpet anarchically, as if deliberately placed to seem messy.

She was beaming up at him.

"You're not a child," Oscar told her, though he was saying it more to himself than to the thing that had masqueraded as his daughter and almost made him kill April.

The control it had had over him… The way it blinded him to what it was doing…

It had been unreal. Oscar had left because of it. The harm that had been done to April… He could not forgive himself for that.

"Won't you come play with me, Daddy?"

"You're not a child," Oscar repeated.

"What are you talking about, Daddy?"

Oscar hated the way she talked. It was so bouncy, as if trying to perform the image of a cheerful child rather than genuinely being one.

How had he ever been so successfully fooled by it?

"You drained the life out of April," he said, directing it at the child, but again, saying it more for his own observation.

"What are you talking about, Daddy?"

"Stop calling me Daddy!"

"But, Daddy—"

"Enough!"

He turned away. He couldn't look at it. The pain this thing had caused, the mental torment, the influence it had over him — it was too much.

He did not want to be influenced by it again. He had to keep reminding himself what it was. He had to say it aloud, to ensure he was acknowledging it; to make sure he knew exactly what this thing was.

"I think you're mad, Daddy."

"You are not a child. You are a demon. Your name is…"

What was its name?

What was the demon's name?

"I think you—"

"Lamia," Oscar remembered. "Your name is Lamia. And you are not real."

Hayley — or, rather, Lamia presenting itself as Hayley — stood.

"Come with me, Daddy," she said.

Oscar did as he was told.

He followed her through the living room and into the kitchen.

"Make me a milkshake, Daddy."

He opened the cupboards, looking for the powder. It was on the top shelf, just where they kept it. He took a glass from the draining board and opened the fridge, taking out the milk.

"Quicker, Daddy."

He sped up. He poured the powder into the glass, poured the milk, and stirred so quickly his arm ached.

What was he doing? Why was he obeying her again? He was tricked before, and he could not understand why he was reverting to old ways.

Yet, even though he was consciously thinking this, even though he knew that he was being controlled, he was still helpless to stop it.

It felt exactly like it did when this demon child had manipulated him before.

He finished making the drink, turned, and handed it to Hayley.

She was no longer alone.

She took the drink and sat at the table beside April.

April had no mouth.

Her eyes stared up at Oscar, terrified, beseeching him to help — but she could not verbally request it. There was just skin where her lips should be, her teeth and tongue concealed by flesh.

Hayley was doing this, Oscar knew it. Hayley was ensuring April could not object, could not beg, could not influence Oscar.

Oscar accepted it.

If this was what Hayley wanted, then this was what she would get.

She slurped down the last gulp of milkshake.

April kept looking at him, kept staring, kept trying to use her eyes to plead for help, to get him to realise that this was all wrong.

Hayley held the glass out to Oscar. "Put this in the sink, Daddy."

"Yes, Hayley."

Oscar took the glass and placed it in the sink.

"Get out a kitchen knife, Daddy. The sharpest one you have."

"Yes, Hayley."

Oscar opened the kitchen drawer, found a sharp knife, and took it out. He held it by his side and looked at Hayley for further instructions.

Hayley grinned at April's wild desperation to speak, and her lack of ability to do so.

She couldn't even make a sound.

Hayley looked back to Oscar, who stood so still and obediently, awaiting her command.

"Now kill Mummy, Daddy," she said.

"Yes, Hayley."

THE PILOT TOLD LORENZO THAT THEY WERE TEN MINUTES away from the airport.

Om looked at Oscar's body, strapped in next to him, empty and still.

Om did not imagine the world had more than hours left. And, even if the world had more than hours — say it had days, for example — in that time this body would bloat, and blood would leak out, and it would be an almost useless vessel for Oscar to return to. The internal organs hadn't worked for a few hours and decomposition had begun. It would not be a body that functioned as Oscar expected it to, and if it was left empty of life for too much longer it may not work at all.

They needed Oscar to hurry.

Om looked up, realising that Lorenzo was glaring at him. Lorenzo quickly looked away when Om caught his eye.

"Tell me," Om said, "have I done something wrong, or is it just me you despise?"

Lorenzo snorted an ironic snort — as if he was saving a witty retort just for himself.

"I did what was needed," Om continued. "Oscar is where he needs to be, doing what he has to do."

"And he may fail."

"He might."

"What then?"

"Then the world will end."

"Exactly — and you are at peace with that. You are happy to accept the deaths of over seven billion people. You are ready to embrace a world of suffering."

"I am ready to accept the world as it is, and as it will be."

"You've given in."

"I have not given in, as I have no war to give in to. I crave nothing, so I lose nothing."

"Whatever."

Om smiled.

"Are you proud?" Lorenzo asked. "I mean, that you helped Oscar in a way we couldn't. Are you proud?"

"Are you proud that you have hidden every supernatural catastrophe the first-world has faced?"

"You are avoiding the question."

Om took a moment.

"I am pleased, not proud. I let go of pride long ago; it does nothing but fuel arrogance and a sense of superiority."

"And is that what I have, a sense of superiority?"

"I have just always wondered… Why cover it all up? Why not just let the world know? Let them see the truth?"

"Because that is not what faith is, and without faith we are nothing."

After a moment of awkward silence, the pilot announced that they had arrived and landed the helicopter. A few priests greeted Lorenzo and helped the body to the plane.

It was astounding, the things this Church could do. Such as landing beside a plane at a busy airport and boarding without passports.

They had power Om had never known, and nor did he need to.

He boarded the plane and found a seat away from the gathering priests. The stares did not bother him, but he thought it was best to keep his distance following his conversation with Lorenzo.

After a few minutes, the plane moved to the runway. It sped up, and they were in the air, aboard a lengthy flight that would take Oscar to The Devil, and would reunite Om with his opponent.

39

THE KNIFE IN OSCAR'S HAND FELT... WRONG.

Like it shouldn't be there.

Yet he felt compelled to hold it. Like he had to hold it, and that he should ignore every sense of irregularity about what he was doing.

April, her mouth covered by skin, stared at him, shaking her head wildly.

Her arms were on the table, and the wood of the table had somehow grown into restraints, fixing over her wrists, keeping her in place.

Hayley smiled up at him, and he felt an overwhelming need to please her.

He stepped forward, toward April.

"That's it, Daddy."

He edged toward her again.

"A little more."

He reached her side, looking down upon the wretched bitch whose life deserved to end.

Wait... the what?

Wretched bitch?

Life deserved to end?

Why had he thought that?

She was not a wretched bitch. She did not deserve death.

Yet, as he looked down upon her, that was all he could think. All his warm feelings of love were there, but in a box at the back of his mind, buried, hidden away.

"Now, Daddy."

He took a clump of April's hair in one hand and tilted her head back, exposing her throat. The skin was clean, stretched, and ready. Such a delicate thing, a human neck. It's so reachable, and so easily destroyed.

He held his knife back, stretching his arm, ensuring he had a large swing, big enough to get some force behind his weapon.

"Hurry, Daddy. It's time."

It was time.

He was ready.

He flexed his fingers to ensure he had a tight grip.

"Destroy her just like I killed Father Jenson."

Oscar swung the knife downwards.

Just as the tip was about to meet April's skin, he stiffened his arm and stopped it.

What did she just say?

She killed Father Jenson?

"Daddy, come on."

Why would a child talk about killing a priest?

He looked at Hayley, horrified at what she had just suggested.

"Why aren't you doing it?"

He remembered.

She *had* killed a priest called Father Jenson. He had attempted to christen her, and she burnt his hand. He had confronted her, and she had murdered him.

"Why are you looking at me like that, Daddy?"

Father Jenson's death had occurred just before she had made Oscar threaten April with a knife.

And that wasn't all she had done either...

"I will *not* ask again, Daddy!"

She made a woman tear her own child apart, and Oscar hadn't even blinked.

She had forced Martin to die trying to drown her.

She drained the life out of April so she could live.

Hayley was not a good child.

In fact, she was not a child at all.

She was Lamia.

And Oscar would not be told what to do by a demon.

"Daddy, I–"

He took the knife from beside April's neck and swung it at Hayley, plunging it into the side of her head.It looked like a child and, finding it difficult to let old habits go, Oscar felt momentarily sick for stabbing a young girl.

But the appearance changed. The child-suit fell and Lamia revealed itself. Snakeskin tail, red eyes and the bare torso of a woman.

Oscar swiped the knife again, plunging it into Lamia's body, and repeated this, again and again and again, and his arm ached but he still did not stop.

Flames sprung from Lamia's body, forcing Oscar to close his eyes and turn his head away.

When he opened them, she was gone.

He was in Edinburgh. Below a church. Somewhere hidden away from God.

He was on his knees, panting.

He looked around.

Someone was behind him.

He ran his hands through his hair, told himself he just had

to persevere, had to go through this, had to endure — then turned to see who it was.

And there he stood, the next torturous reminder of Oscar's many, many mistakes.

"Get up boy," said Father Connor O'Neill, "and stop acting the maggot."

40

DESPITE NOT KNOWING WHERE THEIR OPPONENT WAS, THEA and Henry had a good idea which direction to go in. The streets were full of them. People walking absentmindedly out of homes, out of shops, out of cars. So vacant, yet so determined. They weren't running, but they were striding almost as fast as if they were.

Every single one of them was heading in the same direction.

A few onlookers stared out of their windows, marvelling in both wonder and terror. Watching, but trying to avoid being seen.

A truck driver brought his truck to a sudden stop, stepped out, and walked with them.

A woman ran out after her daughter, begging her to come back inside, insisting they would find her help; she just needed to stay at home.

The girl swiped her nails at the mother's throat, and she fell to the floor, choking. Not quite dead, but wounded enough to struggle for breath.

"What is going on?" Henry asked.

Thea stood still, on the high street of Cheltenham town centre, and watched the many walk past her. The crowd grew bigger the further through town it went.

Thea tried to stay calm and think about this carefully. There must be lots of them because they were close to where they were gathering.

Which meant the leader they were seeking couldn't be far away.

"How are there so many?" he asked.

"Because they have all come here. April is close."

He hesitated, before asking, "Should we find her?"

His question was weak. It was a reluctant question, where he was clearly hoping she said no.

Unfortunately, the answer to his questions was yes.

"The only way we can find her is by following all of them," Thea said.

"But when they are all together — what then? There are too many of them."

This was true.

Thea had done mass exorcisms, but on buildings where the victims were enclosed, and with the help of Oscar, April, Julian and others. With so many of them, and all of them out in the open, it would be difficult.

If they were to follow them, they were likely to follow them to their own deaths.

Then so be it, figured Thea.

The world would end either way, so if this was where the last resistance would be, then that was where it would be.

Besides, she had promised Oscar she would not lose April. She intended to keep her promise as best as she could.

"We just follow," Thea said.

"And what then?"

"Just follow."

Thea had no idea about *what then* — they could deal with *what then* later.

She took a moment to compose herself, then followed the crowd, feeling Henry reluctantly follow her.

They continued through the town centre, through the smaller streets where they all packed together, until they reached the base of a hill.

There were even more of them.

It was no longer a crowd; it was a mass. Hundreds, possibly thousands, marching up the hill until they joined the back of a congregation — at which point they dropped to a single knee.

Thea grabbed Henry and went to turn back. This had been a terrible idea.

Then something grabbed her.

She turned. One of the faces that had been so vacant a moment earlier was now full of rage.

As she looked around, she saw all other faces changing too. All the demons that had been guiding the bodies were taking control of their hosts once again.

Thea tried to shove the hand off, but another gripped her, and another, and another — until they hoisted her into the air, grabbing at every part of her body.

She tried to look for Henry. They had lifted him too. Both of them were being carried overhead, with hands clutching at their legs, their chest, their arms, their throat — she could barely struggle. There was no escaping.

She managed not to panic. The knowledge that they would die when the world ended anyway somehow made their imminent deaths a little less scary.

They carried her up the hill and threw her to the floor.

Henry collapsed next to her.

They both looked up and saw it.

April's body was barely recognisable anymore — it was

was still there as a vessel, but her skin was sagging, like a mask that melted, and her body was peeling. It was like The Devil was emerging from its cocoon into a creature all the more dementedly glorious.

Thea dreaded to think what would happen to April's body once the metamorphosis finished and she was no longer needed. It was already in the process of being discarded — would there even be anything left to save?

Thea took out her crucifix.

Henry did the same.

"Remember, it can't hurt us if we keep up the exorcism rites," she urged him. "Are you ready?"

Henry went to respond, but did not manage, for his crucifix was taken from him.

As was Thea's.

They both floated into the air, The Devil grinning wildly as they did. He raised his arms and the two crucifixes turned to flames, burning to ash that settled into a mound upon the grass.

The Devil opened its arms, and fire flew from its hands.

Thea looked to Henry and, for the first time, had no words of encouragement or comfort.

They held hands, preparing for the worst. Perhaps it was time they accepted their fate.

41

O'NEIL CLICKED HIS FINGERS AND THEY WERE BACK IN OSCAR'S kitchen again. O'Neil sat casually, watching Oscar, the heel of his right foot on his left knee, chewing something.

O'Neil had appeared as a mentor to teach Oscar what it was to be a Sensitive, but turned out to be a fear demon — the actual demon, in fact, that opened Hell and begun the terrors they had spent the last year fighting.

Oscar went to speak, but O'Neil raised his hand and silenced him.

"Watch this," he said, with the same imposter Irish accent he had portrayed before.

April and Julian were suddenly there.

Julian sat next to O'Neil, and April made their beverages. She placed a weak coffee in her place, a strong coffee in Julian's, and a tea with four sugars in front of O'Neil.

"No…" Oscar whimpered.

He had not witnessed this conversation personally, but he knew of it. He knew what was about to happen, and he did not want to see it.

If he'd have been there, instead of gallivanting away on

his own arrogant journey, maybe this conversation would never have taken place.

"Father, you said you had bad news on Oscar," Julian said.

"No, it's not true," Oscar insisted.

"Ah, yes," O'Neil said, ignoring Oscar's protestations. "You are definitely Julian. He told me about you."

"He did?" Julian responded.

"Yes, he did. Always curt and straight to the point."

O'Neil carried on talking, but Oscar shouted over him, drowning him out with cries of, "No, ignore it, it's not true, don't listen!"

"That's me," Julian replied, his face stern, oblivious to Oscar's voice and presence.

"No, please..." Oscar begged.

"You, April, you're a little different," O'Neil said, turning to the love of Oscar's life. "He told me many a thing about you. Some of it wonderful. Some of it not.""Oh?" April said.

Oscar fell to his knees.

He couldn't bear to watch O'Neil tell lies to April that could destroy her affection toward him.

"He said you were beautiful; eyes that could turn a man to stone — and I see that, oh, I do. He told me you are his strength, the reason he searches for answers, and the reason he goes on."

"He did?"

"Yes, but he also said there were some downsides to your character. As there are in all of us."

"Oh?"

"Don't believe it, April," Oscar said, running up to her and shaking her.

She did not react to his touch. No response whatsoever. She remained attentive to O'Neil.

"He said you were weak," O'Neil said, and it was like a dagger had dug into Oscar's chest. "That you let a demon baby into you and let it put you in a hospital bed. He said better women would not have let such things happen."

Oscar couldn't watch this; he couldn't listen to anymore.

He turned and ran out of the kitchen but, as soon as he entered the next room, he was in the kitchen once again, seeing the look on April's face as she bowed her head and felt ashamed.

He ran out of the room again and reappeared once more.

It seemed he could not escape this torment.

O'Neil handed a piece of folded paper to the others.

"He had me write this, then pass it on to you," he said.

O'Neil stood and left.

Julian and April looked at the note. Oscar knew where it would lead them, but he could do nothing to stop them going there.

The kitchen disappeared, and they arrived outside a brown brick house with a perfectly trimmed garden and flourishing flowers. A people carrier on the drive, a basketball net above the garage, children's toys scattered along the lawn.

As soon as April and Julian entered this house, in Oscar's absence, they were entering a different realm. This was the moment that the balance would inevitably shift.

Oscar knew this because he had entered this house to go after them and, without the Sensitives left on Earth, Hell was free to open.

This was the moment he had never witnessed, but the darkest parts of his mind had forced him to imagine.

He could not say this was when everything had went wrong, as everything had been going wrong for a while. But he could say with certainty that this was the ultimate moment; the point at which they could not go back.

This was all because of him.

Because of his mistakes.

Because of his lack of foresight and selfish quest. He and April should have been at home, taking care of each other, but they weren't.

The deaths that have happened because of this moment... So many deaths...

He fell to his knees.

He couldn't do this.

There was no way.

He could not bear to relive these torments, these torturous memories, these moments of his past that provided such pain.

But he had to.

He *had* to.

It was the only way to make up for it. The only way to conquer the anger it sparked inside of him.

So he lifted his head.

He was no longer in front of his house.

He was in Purgatory. This was where he had spoken to Derek, just before he was plunged into Hell to face The Devil, only weeks ago.

Only, it wasn't him stood before Derek.

It was April.

"How do I get to Hell?" she asked.

"April, you are not meant to be here," Derek replied.

And, even though it was another moment he had not witnessed, he knew what it was.

And he knew that, should April have listened to Derek, things would be very different.

THEN

TWELVE YEARS OLD

42

Oscar had learned to be silent.

He could not remember a classroom without Bertrand in it. It seemed that, whenever he went up a year and they divided the class into different classes, Bertrand would end up in his. The time he moved up a set in maths, Bertrand moved up too. When he moved from junior school to senior school, guess who was in his new tutor group?

Bertrand didn't even do that much. In fact, he barely approached Oscar.

He was just always there. Staring. That same cocky, knowing grin.

Oscar was scared that, should he speak, Bertrand would just laugh at him, and everyone else would join in.

So he didn't talk.

Teachers spoke to his parents about his silence at parent's evening. They couldn't figure out why he was so quiet all the time, or why he was so shy. He wasn't shy at home, nor was he ever quiet in his evening drama club, or when talking to relatives. It was just school that he seemed to retreat into himself.

Oscar's class had a talk on bullying a few days ago. These people from a local charity came in and spoke about *victimisation*. It meant that bullies were subtle, that they isolated the vulnerable, that they made you think something was wrong with you.

They said that you should always tell a teacher when you are being bullied.

Oscar had considered this, but he wasn't sure what to tell them. Was he supposed to complain about some kid that kept staring at him? Was he supposed to say Bertrand had somehow made his book go up in flames from across the room when he was six years old?

He had believed it was Bertrand in the back of his mind — but whenever such ideas entered his immediate thoughts, he dismissed them. Even though, deep down, he believed Bertrand had done it; he had spent many years thinking it was not possible. Even in his young mind, which was predisposed to believing in magic and wild figments of the imagination, there was enough rationality to know it could not have been Bertrand.

Then there was that one day, when he was the last one to leave the classroom. He was just leaving the inner door, which led pass the toilets and to the outer door.

He paused, closing that inner door behind him, and saw a face in the glass pane of the door he knew he would have to pass through.

That same grin. That same chubby face. That same cocky facade.

Oscar had to go out that door. It was the only way out.

He could do it. He would be okay. Bertrand had never physically attacked him; all he did was stare. He had never thrown a punch, or even so much as barged into him.

Oscar closed the inner door behind him.

Took a deep breath.

Shuffled forward. Small steps, slowly edging toward the door.

Halfway there, he stopped.

Bertrand hadn't moved.

Oscar couldn't do it.

Bertrand laughed. A loud, bare-faced laugh.

"What's the matter?" Bertrand mocked. "You scared, you dirty piece of shit?"

Oscar could remember thinking, even at such a young age, that Bertrand's words had been strangely aggressive for a child. Most playground insults were petty, often with a sexually derogative insinuation that they were too young to actually understand.

But this declaration that Oscar was a *dirty piece of shit* felt far more adult than it should have done coming out of a twelve-year-old's mouth.

Oscar backed up, reversing into the classroom, shutting the door with one last glance at Bertrand's bloated, arrogant smirk.

"Oscar, are you okay?" came a kind woman's voice from behind him.

He turned around. His teacher, Mrs Bellamy, sat at her desk, looking inquisitively at him.

Oscar just stared at her, wide-eyed, not knowing what to say.

"Oscar, what is it?" she asked.

After no reply was forthcoming, she added, "Why don't you want to go home?"

Oscar still didn't know what to say.

"Come here," Mrs Bellamy said, waving him closer and pushing out a chair beside her desk.

Oscar walked stiffly to the chair and sat on its edge.

"Oscar, I am worried about you," Mrs Bellamy said. "Your

mum and dad are worried, too. You seem ever so quiet. What is wrong?"

Oscar looked into her eyes and realised just how heavily he was breathing.

"Oscar, are you being bullied?"

Oscar looked down.

"Just give me a nod if you are."

Oscar gave a gentle, non-committal nod.

"Would you like to tell me about it?"

Oh, yes. He would. Very much.

But he couldn't.

What was he supposed to say?

"Why don't you just start by telling me who it is?"

Oscar's gaze wandered to the table where Bertrand sat.

His teacher looked at the table and started listing all the children who sat there.

"Is it Jake?"

Oscar shook his head.

"Samuel?"

He shook his head again.

"Harris? Kabib? Christopher?"

Oscar still shook his head.

"Then why don't you tell me, Oscar? I won't say anything unless you are happy for me too, I just want to know who it is."

Oscar stared at the space his bully occupied. Willing the words to his lips. Just two simple syllables, just one simple admission, and he would tell her who it was.

He decided he would. He took in a deep breath, prepared himself to say the name, then said it.

"Bertrand," he said, louder than he intended.

"Who?" Mrs Bellamy asked.

"Bertrand."

"Did you say Bert Land?"

"No, Bertrand. It's Bertrand."

Mrs Bellamy looked confused.

"Are you wasting my time, Oscar? Is this some kind of joke?"

Oscar was taken aback. That was not the reaction he was expecting.

"No," he said. "It's Bertrand. He's been doing it for years."

"Oscar," she said, then paused. "There is no one in this class called Bertrand."

Oscar stared at her, allowing the words to sink in. At first, he thought this was some kind of bizarre occurrence. Then he wondered if he'd been imagining things. Then he considered whether she was bullying him too.

Of course she was. Why wouldn't she want to be in on it? Oscar bet they all had a good laugh about him in the staff room.

He rushed out of the classroom. When he reached the outside door, Bertrand was gone.

In fact, Bertrand was not there again the next day. Or the next day, or the day after that.

Oscar enjoyed this. In fact, he became used to Bertrand not being there, and grew in confidence. Even though he remained introverted and socially awkward, he was no longer the quiet, timid boy he was. He focussed on his GCSE exams, and started talking to others. He even made a friend or two.

But, of course, after the years had gone by and Oscar had found some self-esteem, Bertrand was not gone. He was simply waiting for the perfect time to make his next appearance.

NOW

43

"You were not supposed to do this," Derek insisted. "This was Oscar's task, and Oscar's alone."

"And you think I'm going to sit by and let Oscar die?" April bit back.

Oscar covered his face and shook his head.

He could not bring himself to witness anymore, yet he knew he could do nothing but witness it. Hell would give him no escape.

"Send me to Hell!" April was shouting. "Send me to Hell! I want to go to Hell!"

"Oh, April," Oscar pleaded, knowing that they could not hear him. "You do not know what is going to happen…"

"It's below us, isn't it?"

She threw her fist downwards, and the bright white light beneath her cracked.

"April, please don't do this."

April threw her fist down with her entire body behind it.

"April, you are going to fundamentally end the world because of your stupidity!" Derek objected. "April, this is not what's meant to happen!"

April looked up at him.

"Goodbye, Derek," she said.

She punched the ground and fell, plummeting into the depths of Hell.

The bright white light of the room disappeared.

Oscar closed his eyes and covered his face. He felt wind gushing around him, could see the flames dancing between the cracks of his fingers, could feel the screeching of a thousand souls tortured by a thousand demons all around him, and then — nothing.

Stillness.

The familiar smell of April's shampoo. The smell of her clothes after they had been washed. The smell of her sweat after an exorcism.

She was here, but he knew she wasn't.

As soon as he opened his eyes, he would see her, but not as he wished. It would be in whatever way Hell had presented her, in whatever way would torment him most.

But he was wasting time, standing there, keeping his face covered. Who knew what state the world was in now? Who knew whether April was even still alive?

Whatever it was, he had to face it, and he had to hurry.

He took his hands from his face.

He was in the bedroom where he had kept April fastened to the bed. April was there, only she was not tied to the bed, nor did she look like April.

Her appearance was still that of the pale, dishevelled, tortured April with The Devil inside of her. She perched on the end of the bed, watching Oscar. As if awaiting a reaction. Like they were old friends reunited for a coffee.

Yet The Devil still had that look; that one where he knew he had the power.

"I am so fed up of seeing you," Oscar said. "At what point can we end this stupid, pointless battle?"

"You think it's gone on too long?"

"Yes. I've had enough."

"My boy, I have been waging this war for eternity. You are merely a blip in the history book of this war."

"You seem to think, because you are The Devil, I am not—"

"Call me Lucifer."

"… What?"

"The Devil, it's so tricky to keep saying. I prefer my fallen angel name that your religion provided. Lucifer will do just fine."

Oscar huffed. It was all just words; constant conversation about good and evil and who was stronger. He was not lying when he said he was fed up. He was tired, both physically and mentally, from trying to learn from Om's lessons, from trying to endure the reminders of his mistakes, from constantly trying to retain some kind of hope in a war he could not win.

He wondered what would happen if he just gave up. If he just told The Devil that he'd won. He could have the world. It wasn't all that great, anyway.

But that was exactly what his opponent wanted.

"What do you want?" Oscar said, throwing his arms in the air and looking around the imitation of a room he knew too well. "Really, what do you want? To talk? Or should we fight? How about we throw a few punches, is that what you're after?"

"Not at all."

"Then what do you want from me?"

He felt his entire body lurch forward. He felt his voice break, his eyes grow moist, his breath shorten. This was exactly what his opponent wanted.

Oscar turned around. Grabbed mounds of his hair in his fists.

He needed to stop this petulant arguing. He needed to end this continual struggle. He needed to…

What? What did he need to do?

He had no idea.

He turned back to The Devil. Hands by his side, back straight, fists clenched.

"Are we done with this bit yet?" Oscar asked. "You're making me relive something I've already relived every day for the past few weeks. What, you think showing it to me in your make-believe land will create any more kind of struggle for me?"

The Devil shook his head.

"Then what? What do you want?"

"I want to offer you something."

"There is nothing you can offer me that I want."

"I want to offer you *everything* you want."

Oscar felt certain this was it — the final test. The part Om had anticipated.

The Devil would deliver him Parinirvana.

The Devil would make all his dreams come true.

"I don't want it," Oscar said, though it came out in a whisper.

"You don't?"

"No. I do not."

"Okay. Then walk through to the other side and return to your corpse."

The Devil lifted April's hand and indicated a small ball of fire. The fire expanded, and expanded, until the flames created the outline of door.

A door Oscar had to walk through. Once he reached the other side, he was free.

Then he would have defeated The Devil, and he could return.

Surely, after that, he would have what he needed to win.

He would have defeated The Devil in Hell. He could return with the ability he needed to beat his opponent in his own world.

All he had to do was walk through Parinirvana and come out the other end.

That was it.

"You think this is easy, don't you?" The Devil said. "You think walking through to the other side will be as simple as a Sunday morning stroll?"

"There is nothing you can tempt me with."

A grin responded. "Then why don't you be on your way?"

Oscar turned to the door of flames. Walked toward it. The heat was harsh outside the door frame, but inside of the doorway was cooler. Warm like a sunny afternoon.

He reached out a cautious foot, crossed the barrier with it, and placed it down in the blackness.

He glanced back at The Devil, who had not moved.

He placed his other foot in and stood there, at the beginning of wherever he was going.

He took a breath and walked on, entering the darkness.

THEY LEFT THE AEROPLANE, AND OM FOLLOWED LORENZO, the pilot, and Oscar's body to another helicopter. Lorenzo glanced back at him, as if he hoped that Om would have somehow gotten lost.

But Om would not miss this.

He had spent decades in that temple, knowing it was the only way he could be protected. He was much older now, however, and was ready to go out on his own terms.

He felt a little nervous, but quickly let go of any anxiety he felt. He wasn't going to meet a formidable opponent; he was going to greet an old friend. He was being reunited, not challenged, and that was the way he chose to see it.

After a few minutes in the helicopter, Om wondered where they were going. They just seemed to be flying aimlessly, with no particular location in mind.

"Where are we directed?" he asked Lorenzo.

"We'll know when we see it."

Om was confused but, after looking out of the window at the streets below, he understood what Lorenzo meant.

"This is it," Lorenzo said to the pilot. "Follow the crowd."

A vast crowd walked aimlessly, all in the same direction, until they came to a stop behind a mass of people, all of whom were on one knee, then dropped to one knee themselves.

The helicopter flew over this worshipping crowd until they came to a figure on top of the hill.

"There he is…" Om whispered.

He may be stood inside a mortal woman's skin, but it made no difference — Om would recognise Mara anywhere. Sparks flickered from his palms as he sneered at a young woman and a young man stood in front of him, their crucifixes out, ready to battle.

"Fools…" Om muttered — not antagonistically, but sympathetically. Once, he had thought he could use his religion to fight the most ancient, almighty evil.

How wrong he had been.

Mara simply lifted his arms, and those crucifixes rose into the air and burst into flames.

The woman and man looked at each other, joined hands, and turned back to Mara.

"They are going to die…" Om mumbled to himself.

They were both so young, with so much to learn. He could feel the rage burning inside of them, just as he could feel their hope diminishing.

"Let me out," Om abruptly decided, turning to Lorenzo.

"Are you kidding?" Lorenzo said.

"No, let me out."

"We are not putting this helicopter down until Oscar is awake."

"I did not say put the helicopter down, I said let me out."

Lorenzo rolled his eyes.

"And how would you like us to do that?" he asked.

Om looked around, trying to find some rope or something.

"Just lower the helicopter enough for me to jump out," Om suggested.

"Did you not see what just happened with those crucifixes? We go too low and we'll be set on fire."

"You won't."

"Yes, we will."

Om glanced back out the window at the woman and man. They were cowering.

"They are going to die," Om said.

"They are Thea and Henry, both Sensitives. They made their choice."

"And I made mine."

Without warning, Om unbuckled himself and rushed to the edge of the helicopter, where he perched.

"It's too far!" Lorenzo shouted, but Om ignored him.

Om peered out. He readied to jump, then paused, looking back at Lorenzo — who was staring at him bemusedly.

He wondered why they had come to dislike each other so much.

"I do respect you, you know," Om said.

"What?"

"I am glad we have had this opportunity to work together — to come together and make sure Oscar has the best chance."

Lorenzo swallowed. He hesitated, then finally replied.

"Yes," he said, cautiously. "Me too."

"Thanks to the both of us, Oscar knows what he needs to do, and has a fighting chance."

"Yes. I suppose."

Om gave Lorenzo a nod.

"Good luck," he said, then added, "now let me out."

Om wasted no more time. He dropped out of the helicopter and hung from the landing skid, causing the helicopter to sag to the side.

"Fine!" Lorenzo said and turned to the pilot. "Just let him out!"

The pilot dropped a little, and Om took this as his cue to let go. He fell, his arms flailing, and landed on a hard mound of grass.

The helicopter returned to the air, leaving him alone.

Oscar stepped through the burning door and walked down the black corridor. It was not filled with darkness, but with black. He saw nothing but black beneath his feet, by his arms, and above his head.

But this would end. In the distance was a small ball of white light, growing bigger as he approached. His arm stretched out as he walked closer, wanting it more and more. The white light felt full of joy, while this corridor felt ominous and hopeless.

The white light grew bigger and overcame the black, and he found another door, this time made of bright light.

"Oscar," said a friendly voice beside him.

Oscar turned to find a man stood there. Well-fitted blue suit, trimmed beard, endearing smile.

"Who are you?" Oscar demanded, wondering what trick was next.

"Relax," this man said. "It's over. You've passed through Hell."

"No, I haven't. This is another trick."

"It's not a trick, Oscar. It's an offer."

The man, so calm and cool, smiled suavely at Oscar.

"Who are you?" Oscar repeated.

"Who do you think I am?"

"I don't know, that's why I am asking."

"Who do you think would want to greet you on your way into Heaven? Who do you think would want to come down from the angels and thank you for all that you have given?"

"Are you… Him?"

He nodded.

Oscar shook his head. It couldn't be.

"But I screwed up," Oscar said. "I caused this mess. I don't deserve Heaven."

"Oscar, if anything, you deserve it the most," He said, rushing up to Oscar enthusiastically. He took Oscar's arms, held them, and spoke so passionately that Oscar could not help but be convinced.

"Don't you see? You chose love. Love! Out of everyone in this world, you saved those you care about most. If that isn't my influence, then what is?"

"And now what? You're offering me Heaven? What about everyone else? What about April?"

He smiled a knowing smile — not a mocking one, but a deliberate one.

"April is here," He said.

"No. April is on earth, she is suffering."

"Oscar, please. The Devil took her body. April left it long ago. She is happy. Her soul is free."

"But it can't be."

"You looked into those eyes every day for the past few weeks. Tell me, did you see any of April in there?"

Oscar went to object but couldn't. Honestly, the answer was no. He had seen none of April in there. She hadn't even resurfaced. Either she had been buried deep down, or The Devil had already been rid of her.

"Can I see her?" Oscar asked.

"See her? You can do more than that. You can be with her."

"What?"

"She is here, Oscar. Her soul. Waiting for you to join her. She is free of the body stolen from her, and she is happy."

Oscar did not know what to say. He was amazed. He stuttered, wishing he could articulate his astonishment.

"What about everyone else?" Oscar asked.

"You mean Julian? Derek? Maddie? Even Father O'Neil, who had also freed himself of his body? Yes, their souls are here. They are all waiting for you, and they are so, so proud of you."

Oscar looked stared at Him. Was this actually real?

Was this another torment, or was this really Heaven?

And if Heaven was so perfect, what would be so bad about people dying? Maybe the world ending would be a good thing if this was where everyone ended up?

"What about everyone at home?" Oscar asked.

"Don't worry about them. Their lives are in my hands now, not yours." He indicated the door. "Please, go in and enjoy your blissful eternity."

Oscar stepped forward, cautious yet eager. He passed the bright lights of the door and walked into a driveway.

It was the driveway of his house, but not like he remembered it.

The surrounding bushes had never been so green. The flowers were blooming, the air clean, the sun bright.

He walked toward the house and saw a familiar face trimming a nearby hedge.

"Hello, Oscar," came the real Irish accent of O'Neil; not the fake one put on by a demon. Even though Oscar had never truly met the real O'Neil, he was glad to see a familiar face smiling back at him.

"Hi," he said and walked on, eager to see what was inside the house.

He opened the door and stepped in.

Again, it was his house, but better. It was clean. No cracks in the paint, no bits on the carpet.

He entered the hallway and Derek was there, sat on a chair, his head buried in a book. As Oscar passed, Derek lifted his head, took off his reading glasses and smiled warmly.

"You're finally here," he said, and stood, placing a hand on Oscar's shoulder. "I knew you'd make it."

"Derek... is this real?"

"Oscar, that is why you are such a brilliant man — because you question such things. But you are here now. You are *home*. Please enjoy it."

Derek held his arm out, indicating the kitchen.

Oscar kept walking, and came across Julian, sitting at the table, eating some breakfast.

Even Julian seemed pleased to see Oscar, despite Oscar approaching a little cautiously.

"Oscar!" Julian declared. "Don't be nervous. It's fine."

"But — aren't you mad at me? I failed."

"You never failed. Only I did. You were the strong one, Oscar. You always were."

And then it occurred to Oscar, what Om had spoken about: Parinirvana. The bliss that would be presented to him. To defeat The Devil he had to let go of everything he held onto, and that would be his last test.

But what if it wasn't a test?

What if this was real?

What if this was really Heaven?

"She's waiting for you," Julian said, indicating the backdoor.

Oscar opened the backdoor and stepped into the garden, surrounded by colourful plants and beneath a clear, blue sky.

And there she stood. Unscathed and unharmed.

And happy.

Oh, so happy.

It was April.

And she was free.

46

THEA AND HENRY LEAPT BACK AND GLANCED AT EACH OTHER, startled.

It wasn't every day an ageing Buddhist pushed his way through crowds of the possessed, but here he was. He stood between them and The Devil, who looked down and sneered, squinting, as if trying to recall the face.

He stumbled to the ground, feeling the weight of his age pulling him down. Thea went to help the old man, but he waved her away.

"Please, leave me," he said. "You just keep your distance. Stay behind me, whatever you do."

He forced enough strength to his feeble legs to push himself up to his knees. He felt his back, then closed his eyes and breathed through the pain. He seemed to accept the pain and come to terms with it quickly; he was not prepared to let it stop him.

He turned to the king of Hell.

The Devil said nothing, at first. He stared back at this man with vague recognition, twisting April's head to the side.

Then The Devil smiled a wide, sadistic smile.

"Om Samsara," he said, a deep, grave voice coming out of the fading skin of April's once unblemished face.

"Mara," the man called Om replied with an air of satisfaction.

"What's going on?" Henry asked Thea.

Thea did not know, but she followed Om's instructions and moved back, putting some distance between them, but not too far — they didn't want to enter the crowd of disciplines.

"You left your temple," The Devil acknowledged.

"You left your Hell," Om retorted.

The Devil cackled like this was the funniest joke he'd heard in a long time.

"You pathetic, foolish man. You were safe there. You think your spiritual bullshit will protect you out here?"

"I've not come for protection."

"Then what have you come for?"

This was a good question.

His eyes were young last time they had looked at this entity. Now they were so much older, and he was determined to go out on his own terms. He wished to stand defiantly as he showed that, even in death, he would still not give in to its temptations.

He stood tall and said, "To look into your eyes as I resist you once again."

The Devil's smile turned to a frown of disgust, a contortion of rage; disbelief at Om's daring to oppose him.

"And what have you come armed with?" The Devil asked. "Your lessons? Your faith? Your quest? Tell me, what will an old man like you fight me with?"

"I need not fight you."

"You accept your fate, then?"

"I accept what has happened, and what will happen."

"What does that even mean?"

The Devil lifted out April's fist and Om rose from the ground, lifted inches into the air, where he hovered.

"You won't win," Om said.

"Won't I?"

The Devil opened April's fist, and Om dangled by his throat.

"You'll never win so long as there are those of us who resist your temptations."

"Will never win? Don't you see, my old friend — I already have."

He squeezed his outstretched hand. Finger marks pressed against Om's neck as he suffocated.

Om tried to talk, but couldn't. He tried to get some words out, tried to say something, but the force on his throat was too much.

"What?" The Devil asked.

Om tried to speak again, but failed.

"Can't talk?"

The Devil dropped his arm and Om fell to the floor, grabbing his throat.

"What is it? Whatever do you have to say?"

"Oscar will beat you. He will win."

"Oh, Om. Didn't you hear? Oscar is dead."

"What?" Thea cried out.

Om's head turned, and his eyes met hers.

"Is that true?" she asked. "Is Oscar dead?"

Poor girl. She did not know. Om knew he had to explain.

"Yes, but–" he said, but before he could say any more, his body went up in flames. Within the fire, his arms thrashed and his body wriggled, fighting against a painful death he could do nothing to resist.

It didn't take long until the wriggling stopped, and the

fire ended. Just a burnt corpse was left, covered in blackened clothes.

Thea rushed to the man's side, looking upon a blackened, unrecognisable body.

She looked up at The Devil, who grinned at her.

"Oscar…" she gasped. "No…"

47

OSCAR RAN TO APRIL AND PUT HIS ARMS AROUND HER.

She smelt just like he remembered, and her body fit in his arms just like he recalled.

This was April, exactly as she was before her body had been taken over. Wearing her same unique clothes, her same smile, and with the same happiness she always had when he arrived.

He wanted to burst, such was his affection, such was his pleasure at being reunited. God, he loved her. So, so much. With every cell in his body, he yearned for her, and he had never felt happiness like he felt in that moment.

He kissed her, delicately yet passionately, then pulled his head back and looked at her.

"April, is this really you?" he asked.

"Yes, it is," she answered, so gleefully, just as happy to see him as he was her.

"And are you okay?"

"I am okay."

"But with The Devil in your body, with you being possessed, didn't it hurt? Wasn't it–"

"Oscar, stop. It's okay. I'm okay."

He looked back at her, amazed. She couldn't be. Not after everything she had been through.

But she was.

She was so okay. She had recovered from the ordeal, of course she had, she was strong, and she was now in a blissful place, a place they could spend the rest of *forever.*

"We're together," Oscar said. "I can't believe it, we're together. And we are away from everything. None of it matters anymore, it's just us, no fights, no demons — just us."

She nodded. "It always will be."

He leant his forehead against hers. A gesture that had always meant so much to both of them. It was the reassurance they gave before battle, the hope they passed from one to the other.

"You just have to let go of that life you had before, and then we will be able to stay here forever," she said.

This struck Oscar as a little peculiar.

"We have to do what?"

"Let go, just like Om told you. Let go of that life we had on Earth. Let go of your body, and promise you will never return to it."

"But why would I want to let go of that life? That life is where we met, where we fell in love, where we–"

He stepped back. Looked upon her differently.

All the pain he thought he'd escaped came hurtling back.

How stupid he had been.

Om was right, but not in the way she was saying. She was trying to keep him here, not because she wanted him to be with her — but because she wanted him to be trapped. Unable to go back. By removing any attachment to that world, he would leave The Devil unopposed.

"My God," Oscar said. "You almost had me."

Om had taught him that he must let go of everything; even Parinirvana.

This place wasn't just made by Mara, it *was* Mara.

Mara was temptation. He used everything you were attached to against you, to defeat you; to tempt you away.

That was a perfect imitation of the Heaven Oscar had longed for.

Om was right — Mara was both physical and intrinsic. He was both the entity, and the evil within all of us.

Everything in this place was provoking the emotions that allowed The Devil to win.

He had to let go of all of it — only then would he be able to defeat The Devil. Even if it was temporary. Only then would he have nothing The Devil could use to attack him.

But he allowed himself another moment. Despite the suffering occurring in his world, the pain and torture, he allowed himself another minute, just to pretend that this was April.

"What's the matter?" she asked — or, at least, this perfect imitation of her asked.

"I have to let go of you."

"But I love you. Don't you love me?"

"It is because I love you that I must let go."

"I — I don't understand."

He stepped toward her. Gazed upon the face identical to hers, and wished he could kiss it one more time, even though it was fake.

He reached out for her hand and held it.

"Everything that has happened is because of how attached I am to you — because of how much I love you. To save you, that has to end."

"Oscar, you are talking nonsense."

"Goodbye, April."

He dropped her hand.

Stepped back.

He closed his eyes and emptied his body of everything he loved.

His friends.

His life.

And her.

April.

He refused to love her, refused to give in. Refused to accept a wonderful eternity that would be so ideal, should it have been real.

Once April was gone, he felt the world around him go too.

He fell, falling downwards into an abyss. Just as he was about to make an impact with something, he jolted.

He heard an engine. The spinning of a rotor blade. The sound of a familiar voice telling him to wake up.

When his eyes opened, he was in a helicopter, and Lorenzo was looking at him.

THEN

FIFTEEN YEARS OLD

OSCAR WASN'T PARTICULARLY GROWING UP TO BE WHAT ONE would refer to as a ladies' man. In fact, he was growing up to be an awkward recluse. Yet, what some may see as off-putting and socially weird, a girl may occasionally see as awkwardly charming.

This had been the case with Gemma.

Oscar had been too scared to approach Gemma, and she had been too scared to approach him. They weren't the most confident individuals. In fact, they barely spoke. Occasion-ally, they would be forced to answer questions in class, which would be a moment they'd dread, and would cause them waves of anxiety that no one else seemed to get.

In this way, they seemed to bond. Any time they were asked a question and forced to answer, whether it be in Maths, English, Science or whatever other lesson they were in, they would always save a smile for each other. As soon as they'd given their answer and breathed a sigh of relief, they'd look over and see the other smiling at them reassuringly. As if that person was the only one who got it — the only one who understood just how scary it was to have to speak aloud in front of class.

It wasn't until the teacher put them together in science that they spoke properly. This moment of ingenuity, by a teacher completely unaware of what luck they had just created, was enough for them to engage in conversation and find out just how much they had in common.

Thus, it was arranged, that the following Friday, they would go to the cinema.

Oscar spent the entire week both looking forward to Friday, and dreading Friday. He changed his mind multiple times about what he'd wear and about how much wax he'd put in his hair. He tried to think of conversations he could begin, and he even wrote a few topics on the back of his hand so he'd remember them should there be an awkward silence he wished to fill.

He wondered whether she was as scared as he was.

When they met each other outside the cinema, both on time, he felt the dreaded nerves sink into his belly. He felt sick. He willed himself to turn back, to not go through with this, to just go back home and watch television.

But he didn't. He went through with it. They made introverted small talk and, finding comfort in their mutual anxiety, they went into the cinema and watched the movie.

The movie itself was about a young boy who turned into a zombie. It wasn't a conventional horror, however, as he fell in love with another girl. This both intrigued and annoyed Oscar. He loved zombie movies and disliked when a film messed with conventions he loved — yet, at the same time, he was pleased that it had both elements of horror and romance, as this would satisfy both of them. Gemma really seemed to like romance.

He became engrossed in the movie and soon forgot that

he was on a date. He willed himself to move his hand to hers, to just place it on the armrest and inch forward and reach out, but he did not have the confidence to do so.

He tried building up to it but, amid his mental determination, he saw something that drew his attention.

A few rows in front of him. The back of a head. Big, with chubby skin and messy hair.

It looked familiar.

Oscar told himself it wasn't possible. He hadn't seen him for years. It was ridiculous.

He doesn't exist, remember?

Except, he didn't really believe that. It hadn't just been childish imagination. He had seen Bertrand every day for years.

Yet, he hadn't seen him again since he was twelve.

It was just a boy who looked alike.

This boy's head turned to whisper something to the person next to him. In the darkness, his features were covered in shadow, and Oscar couldn't make them out. He only had a partial side-on view and there was no way to know for sure.

Oscar told himself to stop being stupid.

It wasn't him.

Still, the inescapable feeling of dread had risen through him. He was no longer thinking about how to hold Gemma's hand, or what he could say to her. He was thinking about Bertrand, and whether he was here, and whether he was back.

He decided he was being ridiculous. This boy was not Bertrand, he was just a boy.

When the film finished, Oscar tried to see if he could see the boy's face, but he had already gone.

"What did you think?" Gemma asked.

Oscar didn't understand what she was asking at first. His attention had not been on the movie for the last twenty minutes.

"Yeah, it was good," he said, no idea whether it was.

They left the cinema in silence. Oscar wanted to make conversation, and he could feel her glances; she wanted to talk, too.

But his mind was elsewhere.

And, as they exited the cinema and entered the low light of late evening, he saw a figure across the street.

Watching him.

Features masked by shadow, and no way for Oscar to be sure... but, in his mind, it was unmistakable.

Oscar froze. Stared. His heart raced; his body tensed.

"Oscar?" Gemma said. "Are you okay?"

He didn't hear her.

The figure walked forward, out of the shadow. The lack of light still made it difficult to see but, the more he approached, the more he looked like him.

A van drove past, blocking Oscar's view and, when it had left, the figure was gone.

Oscar looked around, searching for what he was convinced he'd seen.

He told himself that Bertrand wasn't there, and he turned back to Gemma.

But it wasn't Gemma standing there anymore.

"You scared?" he asked.

"Huh?"

Oscar's entire body trembled.

"I said, are you scared, you dirty piece of shit?"

Bertrand placed his fingers against Oscar's skull and a pounding headache overcome him. It felt as if his brain was expanding, like his skull was shaking, and he couldn't think.

It became too much and, with one last look in the eyes of the strange boy who had just returned, he collapsed to the floor.

He woke up in hospital a few hours later.

NOW

49

As Oscar opened his eyes, he felt different. Sluggish. Like everything was delayed. His muscles were dead weights, his bones were stiff to move.

He went to sit up, but a hand pushed him back down.

"Just take a minute," said Lorenzo. "You can fight, but just wait a minute."

"I don't have a minute–"

"Please, you need to listen. Just wait."

Oscar reluctantly lay back down.

He wanted to get up; he wanted to fight — he wanted to take the power he had gained and face The Devil. This was the best chance he had.

But he felt awful. The body felt heavy. Rigid. It stunk.

"I imagine you aren't feeling particularly great," Lorenzo observed.

"Uh huh," Oscar grunted, closing his eyes and willing away a headache.

"Your body has been a corpse for almost a day now. It has already started decomposing. Your organs aren't going to work properly."

"Well that's going to be great story to tell my grandkids."

Lorenzo's head dropped.

"Oscar, there — there is something you weren't told. Something not explained to you, for fear that you wouldn't go along with this had you known."

"Oh, more bad news? What is it — my headache won't ever go? My body will always feel like death?"

Lorenzo bowed his head and sighed. Deliberated, clearly struggling over what he had to say to Oscar.

"Just tell me," Oscar said, starting to feel his sense of touch return. His fingertips felt delicate, and his brain felt like it was the wrong size for his skull.

"This is temporary," Lorenzo said.

"What is?"

"This body. It won't last a lifetime. It will expire quicker."

"So, what do I have? Just twenty more years? Ten?"

"You have hours."

Oscar stared back at Lorenzo.

Did he just say hours?

Oscar went to speak but did not know what to say.

"This body you are in is a corpse, Oscar. Not a living thing. The heart hasn't beaten in a day, the lungs haven't been used — it is like trying to fix a machine with faulty equipment. It may chug along, but eventually..."

"I will stop chugging," Oscar said.

"Precisely."

Lorenzo looked away.

He wasn't sure whether to be angry for not being told this, or stupid for not figuring it out himself. Of course his body wouldn't work as it had. Why didn't he think of it?

In a way, it wasn't so bad. If he hadn't left his body he'd have died anyway, along with the world.

But despite how much he tried to rationalise it with himself, it did not relieve the anger. And, to make it even worse, he knew he needed to let go of that anger — he had just endured Hell to overcome negative emotions, and he had to repress his reaction or it would all be for nothing.

He covered his face and huffed. With everything Oscar had already given, his shortened life felt like the nastiest gift yet. Should he rescue April, he would not get to spend his life with her. He would not watch their children grow up, not kiss her on their wedding day — he wondered if he'd even get to say goodbye.

If he saved her, how much longer would he last? How would he tell her?

And here it was. The real reason he had to let April go.

Not just because that meant letting go of the Mara within…

But because that was the only way he could do this.

He willed the thoughts away and tried to let go.

Let go of April. Let go of the life he wished to live. Let go of everything he would never get to do.

Despite his body aching, he felt mentally strong. He felt able to take on anyone.

Including The Devil.

He leant up, batting away Lorenzo's hand as it reached out to support him. He looked out of the window.

He saw her below. April. Skin sagging off her bones and red in her eyes. Stumps of two horns were beginning to show. She was slowly disappearing, and The Devil was taking prominence.

The charred remains of a Buddhist monk lay dead on the ground.

Thea and Henry cowered on the floor.

He couldn't wait any longer. He couldn't dwell on what could happen, nor could he second guess the strength he had gained. He had to face the opponent.

"Let's do this," Oscar said, with less conviction than he wished to have.

"Let's lower the helicopter," Lorenzo instructed the pilot.

"No — not here. Take me further along. I want to surprise him."

"Move further along," Lorenzo told the pilot.

The pilot flew the helicopter away.

50

"See?" The Devil said, pointing at the helicopter as it disappeared. "They know Oscar is dead. They know it's over. They are escaping — saving themselves like anyone sensible would do."

Thea and Henry were on their knees. Weeping. Holding each other.

There was no point running. Where would they go?

There were hundreds to thousands of disciples surrounding them, spreading to the bottom of the hill. They couldn't run through them.

And in terms of fighting…

There was no fight anymore. The Devil had sent their crucifix up in flames. Their only weapons had been their crucifixes and the exorcism rites — neither of which wielded any power over The Devil anymore; not with the strength The Devil had gained.

The only thing they could do was hold onto each other and hope for a quick death.

They had tried, and they had done so knowing the odds

were against them, knowing that there was little they could do; knowing the battle was unlikely to be won.

Oscar had tried, and he had failed. They held no grudges against him for that. They knew that he'd have done the best he could do — but the hope that he had succeeded diminished.

The only thing left to do was to accept their fate.

"I'm sorry," said Thea quietly to Henry.

"What? What are you sorry for?"

"This is all my fault."

"It isn't."

"You were going to leave, going to spend your last moments with your family. And I stopped you. Foolishly saying that there was hope, that we had a chance, that we have to keep fighting. And now look at us..."

"Thea–"

"You could have been with your family. Instead, you are stuck here with me, about to die for nothing."

Henry grabbed hold of Thea's cheeks, lifted her face, and looked her dead in the eyes.

"I regret nothing," he said. "If there is a place to spend our last moments, it is here with you."

Thea smiled solemnly.

She took hold of his hand in hers, gripping it.

"Come on," she said, standing, pulling him to his feet. "Let's do what we intended to do. Let's go out fighting."

They both turned to The Devil, who watched them with a mocking smirk.

He was always smiling, and it was always sinister. Grinning or smirking or beaming with such arrogance.

"What's this?" The Devil asked. "Two Sensitives ready to die together?"

"Fuck you," said Thea. "Do your worst."

Another grin. "As you wish."

The Devil readied April's fists, flames flickering, conjuring a stream of fire.

So they would be burnt alive. That was how they would die.

They stood defiantly.

Thea tried not to think about the pain they were about to endure. She tried not to wonder how much agony she would suffer before it killed them, and endeavoured not to ruminate about the indignity of the prolonged anguish.

The Devil prepared to aim.

Thea closed her eyes. Flinched. Readied herself.

Waited.

And waited some more.

The fire didn't come.

She was still alive.

She opened her eyes to see Henry looking back at her, thinking the same thing.

They looked toward The Devil, who was now on his knees, as if he had just been kicked over. Embers flicked from his fists to the grass.

He looked beyond angry. He was furious. Livid at the impudence.

"Who dares?" he roared.

He stood, fire flicking from his palms, a snarl across his face. Thea hadn't seen this look before — it was the look of disbelief.

Someone was being defiant.

Someone didn't realise when they were defeated.

Thea was not grateful. She just wanted her death to be over.

Then she saw a silhouette approach from behind The Devil.

A spark of hope fluttered within her.

"Tell me your name," The Devil demanded. "I want to know before you die."

"Forgive those who trespass against us," said the man, holding a crucifix out before him. "Lead us not into temptation, but deliver us from evil!"

The man lunged held out his crucifix, and The Devil fell to the ground once more.

Thea saw the face and could not believe it.

It wasn't true. He wasn't dead.

He was here.

He was alive.

He stood over The Devil, and this time he was the one grinning.

"To answer your question," he said, "my name is Oscar — and it's time to send you back to where you came from."

5 1

The Devil stood, throwing his arms into the air, soaring fire into the sky. He turned this fire and aimed it at Oscar.

Oscar held his crucifix high and kept his body behind it. The flames rebounded away, leaving him unscathed.

"How..." The Devil gasped.

"You don't affect me anymore."

Oscar knew that when The Devil cannot fight externally, they would fight internally — so Lucifer turned his attention to what he knew would destroy Oscar.

He grabbed the skin of April's face and pulled it upwards, contorting it like he was moulding a piece of clay. He pulled on her arms, distorting the skin from her body.

Oscar strode toward him. He remained impervious to The Devil's attempt. Let go of what he was attached to. Resisted temptation.

The Devil wished to tempt him into anger, into losing control — but Oscar did not give into temptation.

And it wasn't just The Devil's large, grand attempts at temptation he resisted — it was all the smaller ones, too.

Impatience. When they took on St Helen's Psychiatric Unit too soon, and Maddie died.

Obsession. When Hayley had become more than a daughter — she had become his every fixation.

And wrath. Watching April's body degrade every day as The Devil grew in power, feeling helpless to stop it from happening.

He no longer gave into temptations of impatience, obsession and wrath.

And he would not give into his desperation to save April's body, or irritation that The Devil persisted by hurting the one he loved, or sadness that April may not return to this world the same, should she return at all. The only way to save April would be to remain impervious to The Devil's torment of her.

And, for this reason, The Devil found that there was no way it could beat Oscar.

But the question was not whether The Devil could beat Oscar — but whether Oscar could beat The Devil.

"Disciples," The Devil commanded, standing tall. "Begin."

All those bodies surrounding the hill stood from their position on one knee. The demons emerged onto the faces of those they inhabited. The evil that surrounded the remaining Sensitives grew.

Thea looked at Oscar, worried.

Oscar threw her his crucifix.

"Fight them off," he said.

"What?" Thea exclaimed. "How? There are too many!"

Oscar shook his head. "Not for someone like you."

"But, Oscar–"

"You've done mass exorcisms before, you know you can do it."

"Not with this many. I can't exorcise–"

"I don't need them exorcised; I just need them out of the way."

Thea went to object again but, seeing the resilience on Oscar's face, she did not.

Oscar worried for a moment whether she could handle the task — but he had faith in her. Besides, he could not concentrate on his battle if he was worrying about hers.

So he turned away from her, trusting that she could achieve what she needed to.

He returned his focus to Lucifer, who hid behind the face of April, the thief who endeavoured to take a world he did not belong to, and did not belong to him.

It was time for this to end.

"Leave," Oscar said.

"Leave?"

"This is not your world."

Lucifer's face twisted into rage.

"This *is* my world if I wish to take it!"

Oscar shook his head. He straightened his arms out, making the shape of a cross out of his body.

"For haughty men have risen up against me, and fierce men seek my life," he continued, citing the rites of exorcism he had used so many times before.

"You think this will work against *me?*"

Oscar nodded. "Yes. Yes, I do."

52

"I DON'T NEED THEM EXORCISED; I JUST NEED THEM OUT OF the way."

Thea looked at Henry, who stared back at her, awaiting guidance.

She took a deep breath. Held it. Let it go.

He was looking at her with such vulnerability, such fear. She felt exactly the same — but she knew, for the sake of their task, she had to hide it. She had to show him nothing but strength, even if it was feigned strength.

"We've done this before," Thea said.

"There weren't this many."

She smiled. Placed a hand on his shoulder.

"We weren't this strong."

He held her stare, then gave her the gentlest of nods. A nod she interpreted as — *okay, let's do this.*

She turned to the oncoming possessed, the demonic infestation of humankind. The horde of them, so many she could not see the end.

She took in another deep breath. She could do this. She could. She so could.

I'm screwed.

She held the crucifix high. Told herself not to think such foolish thoughts. April was the one who always believed in her, and if Thea would not give this her all for the sake of the world — she would do it for April.

She gripped the crucifix, its edges digging into her hand and causing a twinge of pain; a twinge of pain she ignored.

"Turn back the evil upon my foes," she said, looking at one face, then turning to another. "In your faithfulness, destroy them."

"Hear us, oh Lord!" Henry responded, unprompted.

The first row of possessed faltered, but temporarily. They glanced at one another, not so much a look of *oh shit*, but a look of *what's this bitch doing?*

They doubted her.

This spurned her on further. They would soon realise how much people pay when they doubt her.

"Because from all distress you have rescued me, and my eyes look down upon my enemies."

"Glory be to the Father!"

They stumbled a little. They did not back away, but they did not persist. They hovered, waiting to see what her next move was, expecting an act of power.

Thea tried to think — how had they exorcised St Helen's Psychiatric Unit? She had performed a mass exorcism that night — how had she done it?

Three Sensitives had formed a triangle around the building, each of them saying the prayer, and Thea had...

Thea had entered the building. She had walked amongst the possessed. She had used her gift from inside the building.

She'd had to be among the possessed to succeed.

She turned to Henry and thrust the crucifix into his hands.

"You remember the rites of exorcism?" she quickly asked.

"Uh huh, I think so."

"Then do it."

She stepped forward, striding toward the crowd.

"What are you doing?" Henry cried out. "They will kill you!"

Thea looked back. Smiled.

"Not if you keep going," she said.

He went to object, but she decided not to let him. She ran onwards, disappearing between the bodies.

"Fill your servants with courage to fight manfully against that reprobate," Henry continued, and Thea listened as long as she could, but his voice faded quickly.

Thea pushed aside the first few lines of possessed, barging them out of the way, mining further, until she could see nothing but demented faces, and feel nothing but outreaching arms.

She knocked their arms out of the way. Strode onwards, persisting forward.

She kept going until she was in the middle of them, surrounded.

She stood still, waiting to feel her power surge through her.

53

"I COMMAND YOU, UNCLEAN SPIRIT!" OSCAR BELLOWED, screaming like he never had; screaming like he knew it would be the last time he ever screamed it. "Along with all your minions now attacking this servant of God!"

"You think this works?" The Devil said, approaching Oscar, slowly edging forward. The arrogant facade had faded a little, but there was still plenty of self-belief behind that stride.

"By the mysteries of the incarnation, passion, resurrection and ascension of our Lord!"

The Devil advanced until he was a few steps away.

Oscar saw Thea disappear into the crowd as Henry gently spoke the words of prayer. He hoped she knew what she was doing.

"I command you to obey me to the letter!" Oscar boomed. "I am a minister of God despite my unworthiness!"

The Devil grinned. The initial shock Oscar had provoked, the surprise at his strength — it seemed to pass.

He was no longer phased, and Oscar could not understand why.

Hoping it was a temporary fault, Oscar persisted.

"Nor shall you be emboldened to harm in any way this creature of God!"

He held his arms out, rigid, firm in the cross he was creating. He did not need a crucifix. He would *be* the crucifix.

The Devil still advanced, until he paused, inches away, close enough that Oscar could see the yellow stains on April's teeth and feel the tepid breath from between her lips.

Oscar held his hand out, placing it on April's forehead, feeling the heat of Hell against his palm.

"They shall lay their hands upon the sick and all will be well with them."

Was April in there? Was she fighting too? Could she hear him?

Come on, April. I need your help. This is it.

"May the Lord, through the merits and intercessions of His holy apostles, show you favour and mercy."

The Devil reached out a hand and pressed it around Oscar's throat. He flexed April's fingers, and the ends of her long, cracked nails dug into his skin.

"I give not into your temptations, Devil," Oscar said, spitting each word coolly, yet full of detest.

"How long will an already dead body take to die again?" The Devil asked.

The Devil squeezed, pressing April's fingers inward, applying force to Oscar's neck.

Oscar struggled to breathe.

He was confused. Terrified. What was going on? This was not meant to happen…

He'd shown up, and he'd commanded power over his enemy.

He'd acquired this strength.

He'd resisted the temptation to feel anger, hostility, worry… yet The Devil still had a hold over him.

But why?

What was it that The Devil still held over him?

He could feel it, but he couldn't explain it. There was still a piece of The Devil inside of him, still some way he'd wriggled into his mind. There was one last piece of temptation that he needed to remove.

But what was it?

He'd endured all the torment in Hell, he'd done all that. He had no idea what he had left.

"You see, my boy," The Devil spoke. "Whatever you call me — The Devil, Lucifer, Mara… There is no greater power than that name."

Oscar grabbed hold of April's arm and tried helplessly to push it off.

"You can let go of everything you hold dear."

The Devil squeezed harder. Oscar felt his throat crush.

"You can resist every temptation."

Oscar felt his mind fade.

How was The Devil doing this? What had Oscar failed to overcome?

He had done everything he needed to do…

"But as much as you try," The Devil said, "I have been preparing for this moment all your life. And you can *never* let go of a childhood where all you ever knew was fear."

The Devil threw Oscar's body to the floor and stood over him, his fists burning with flames, getting ready to end the life of his most formidable opponent.

He placed April's fading face an inch from Oscar's and asked a question Oscar did not expect to hear:

"What's the matter? You scared, you dirty piece of shit?"

Oscar's eyes widened.

Oh, dear God.

Finally, he realised how The Devil still had hold of him.

Oscar had thought The Devil's attack started a year ago,

but he was wrong. It had started when Oscar was just four years old.

With eyes of terror, Oscar looked up at the eyes of The Devil, and the eyes of the boy who had destroyed his childhood.

"That was you?" he gasped.

THEN

SIXTEEN YEARS OLD

54

THEY SAID OSCAR WAS SMART. THEY SAID HE COULD DO anything with his life. They said the world was laid out for him, and he could fulfil whatever vacancy the world had.

His parents also said he disappointed them. They also said they couldn't understand why he had stopped putting effort into his GCSE exams. They could not understand why his application to work at the checkouts in the local supermarket was the only application he was filling in.

"What about college?" they said.

"What about considering university?" they said.

"Or maybe even an apprenticeship?" they said.

Not that Oscar was averse to any of those things; it was just that they didn't appeal to him. They did not interest him. It wasn't where his focus lay.

To his parents, this was a grave disappointment. But Oscar's spent all his time trying to find out who that boy was.

Who Bertrand was.

Why he was there and why he kept tormenting him.

It became an obsession.

He used his study leave to work, rather than revise. He

would end his shift, and walk home from another eight hours where his body had been working but his mind had been elsewhere.

He'd arrive home and his parents would plead with him to revise, to make some kind of effort to at least get a few grades at his GCSEs. They just wanted a response from Oscar that resembled caring.

But Oscar's attention was elsewhere.

He went on the computer and searched for all the searches he thought might be relevant:

Non-existent child bully.

Tormentor who's not really there.

Terrorised by recurring boy.

There was nothing. Just nonsense about supernatural things such as ghosts and apparitions. People with extreme beliefs in the dead coming back to hurt us.

Was that what Bertrand was? Something evil from a paranormal realm?

He scoffed. Leant back in his chair and ran his hands over his face. He was tired. He'd been thinking about this boy non-stop, and he worried that it was making him mad.

He logged off and went to bed, where he lay awake, unable to sleep.

He never did sleep much. He'd hear things — or, at least, he thought he heard things. He'd even found himself at the doctor's after admitting to his father he'd heard people whispering in his ear in an empty room.

They prescribed him medication.

Those pills became his salvation. Any time he thought he heard something, or felt this overwhelming panic come over him, or let his mind stray to Bertrand, he would take another. And another. And another until he was numb and void of feeling.

His mind strayed from Bertrand. It was as if his medication made him resistant to the torment of this individual.

In fact, he only saw Bertrand one more time.

He'd just finished his English exam. He was sure he'd failed. He had put little effort into the essay. He'd had to discuss how Austen's writing of Mr Collins' letter vividly revealed the character of Mr Collins.

He could not care less.

Not that he disliked books. Quite the contrary, in fact, he enjoyed reading — but he read modern texts about zombies and vampires and wizards. He could not understand why they were forced to read outdated texts about Elizabeth Bennet and Darcy. Who cared whether they ended up together?

As the exam left his thoughts and his mood changed from annoyance to no longer caring, he found his way to the bathroom.

Like most school bathrooms, it was in an awful state. The school had spent a lot of money improving the bathrooms, which had turned out to be pointless. It took only weeks until the walls were once again covered in graffiti, the locks had been broken, and the toilet seats were hanging off.

He entered a cubicle. Locked the door.

The strip light above him flickered.

He looked up, then tried to ignore it.

The strip light flickered again, accompanied by a buzz. When it finished flickering, it stayed on, but dimmer, allowing only a little light.

Oscar flushed the toilet and went to leave the cubicle, struggling to see what he was doing in the darkness.

As soon as he opened the door, his body trembled.

The silhouette of Bertrand stood before him.

"No…" Oscar whimpered.

Why?

Why was he here?

Why was he always here?

Oscar just wanted to be left alone. He wanted to be granted peace, to live his meaningless life without interference.

But he always showed up. Always.

Bertrand stepped forward and Oscar reversed back into the cubicle.

The strip light flickered again.

Bertrand grinned.

"What's the matter?" he asked. "You scared, you dirty piece of shit?"

Upon the repetition of this question, something changed in Oscar. He wasn't sure what it was, or how it happened. Perhaps he'd just become fed up of being asked this question. Perhaps he'd decided his life meant so little that it didn't matter if Bertrand was to kill him.

Or, perhaps, and this was just a possibility — Oscar realised that he had nothing to lose, and there was nothing Bertrand could do to him any longer.

What, was Bertrand going to take away his job? His life? His friends?

He could have them.

But, should he take those things from Oscar, it would be unlikely he'd find much to salvage among them. Oscar felt nothing for his job, he did not cling onto his life, and he had no friends to speak of.

"Leave," Oscar said, quietly, but with a little force to his voice.

Bertrand frowned.

This was the first time Oscar had ever seen him frown. In fact, it was the first time Oscar had ever seen him not grinning.

"Leave!" Oscar said, louder this time, and with more conviction.

Bertrand snarled.

"Leave me alone!"

Oscar pushed Bertrand out of the cubicle, knocking him against the wall.

"I have nothing you can take from me," Oscar said, pushing Bertrand further. "You do not scare me anymore."

Oscar pushed again, and Bertrand fell to the floor.

Bertrand lifted a hand and grabbed onto Oscar's wrist. Oscar felt his arm burn, but he tolerated it. It was nothing. Just a twinge. He could withstand it.

Oscar crouched over Bertrand, confidently frowning into his empty, angry eyes.

"You do not tempt me to feel anger. You do not tempt me to feel fear. And I have nothing you can touch."

Bertrand gripped harder.

"Leave me, and leave this place," Oscar said. "And never come back."

Bertrand squealed, then faded. A tinge of smoke rising from the place on the floor he had occupied.

Oscar wasn't entirely sure what he'd seen. Honestly, he saw a lot of strange things his psychiatrist told him wasn't there. But he accepted it — as far as he was concerned, Bertrand was a part of his imagination, and this was his imagination killing him off.

So he left, satisfied. It was gone, and a childhood of torment was finally over. There followed the happiest few hours he'd had in a long time.

The happiness didn't last, and his anxiety returned. He'd see things out of the corner of his eyes, or hear things as he walked through an empty street. He put it down to craziness and swallowed his pills.

He decided he was nothing and wasn't worth the time or

effort a psychiatrist might give him. He resolved himself to spend his days living his meaningless existence, caring little for where it took him.

Two years later, a woman called April would meet Oscar in a pharmacy and change everything.

NOW

55

Oscar looked up at The Devil, unable to believe the words just spoken by the epitome of evil.

"Are you scared, you dirty piece of shit?"

"That was you?"

Oscar shook his head, defiant in The Devil's smiling grimace.

"No... It can't be..."

The Devil stood, straightening his back, like he was preparing for a cocky strut.

"That was you?"

The Devil nodded.

"Why?"

"We knew who you were," The Devil replied. "We knew what we needed to do."

"What you needed to do?"

"Remove any ambition. Any drive. Ensure you became nothing."

Everything made sense.

Bertrand had spent Oscar's childhood doing whatever he

could to remove any confidence. He systematically isolated him, making sure Oscar did not make friends. He removed Oscar's self-esteem piece by piece. By the time Oscar was sixteen, he was nothing. He did not want to become anything, and he was happy staying that way.

Bertrand had created a person who would be least likely to stand up for what he believed in, never mind attempt to save the world. He had created a weakened enemy.

All for this moment.

Somehow, Hell had known what Oscar could become — they had known he would be the world's last defence. So they had destroyed him.

Until April came along.

Until the love of his life showed him he was not the person Bertrand had created.

Oscar knew he could not be that scared little child anymore.

He could not be that terrified boy who was too scared to tell April how he felt.

He could not be that weak man who allowed a demon child to control him.

He could not be the pathetic mess of a person Bertrand had created — not now.

Not anymore.

"You have failed," Oscar stated.

"Excuse me?"

Oscar pushed himself to his knees.

The Devil went to send the flames he had conjured in Oscar's direction, but Oscar resisted with a defiant, "No!"

The Devil looked peculiarly at Oscar.

"These childhood fears you refer to…" Oscar said. "You failed."

"I failed?"

"You tried to create a person who would never stand up to you. Who would never beat you."

"Hah! Just because you grew up and had a few friends, you you've changed?"

"If I was not a threat, you wouldn't have bothered."

"It was a precaution. As long as you are alone, you are nothing."

The Devil lifted his fists of fire into the air once again.

Oscar considered those words: *As long as you are alone, you are nothing.*

He looked at Henry. So terrified, speaking the rites of exorcism with an unmistakable tremor in his voice. Everything about him screamed fear.

But he was still there, and he was fighting for Oscar, and the world.

He peered into the crowd of the possessed. Thea was among them. He could feel it. He could see the demons cowering away from her strength. She had never taken on such numbers, or such powerful opponents.

But she was still there, fighting for Oscar and the world.

And finally, he looked into the eyes of The Devil.

But they weren't The Devil's eyes. The Devil was in there, but he was only using those eyes.

They were actually April's eyes. And he looked deep into them, searching them, trying to find her. Seeking her presence.

And he could see her.

Hidden away.

She was too strong to be concealed. That look of devotion she would always give him was covert, but he could see it.

She was still in there. Fighting for Oscar. And the world.

She had helped create the person Oscar was. Through her

affection, she had undone all of Bertrand's work. Through her love, he had gained the strength to lead — a strength he never had as a boy.

And the effect that April had on him was something The Devil could never have predicted. Something made of pure evil could never understand what impact the love of another person could have.

"Leave," demanded Oscar.

"What?" retorted The Devil.

"Leave!" Oscar said, with more power. He pushed into the centre of April's chest, knocking The Devil backwards.

The Devil snarled.

"Leave us alone!"

The Devil tried raising his fists, but the fire flickered to ambers.

"I have nothing you can take from me."

Oscar pushed him back again. The Devil cowered, backing away, recognising these words — knowing that he was about to lose.

"You do not scare me anymore."

Oscar pushed The Devil again, this time knocking him onto his back. He stood over his opponent, seeing the greatest evil, the king of Hell, the most formidable opponent he had ever faced — shrinking. Cowering. Trembling.

Oscar resisted all the temptations The Devil had given him. He held strength over Lucifer that could not be touched.

There was no Mara left in him, and soon there would be no Mara left in this world.

"You do not tempt me to feel anger. You do not tempt me to feel fear. And I have nothing you can touch."

Oscar placed his fingers against The Devil's temple.

"Leave me, and leave this place."

The Devil screamed, pain in his shriek.

"And never come back."

Oscar pressed his fingers harder against April's head.

The Devil screeched and wailed and shouted, until a fiery light surrounded them, and they both disappeared from this world.

56

THE ROOM WAS LIKE A BOX. IT WAS EMPTY OF CONTENTS AND void of colour. A strange feeling accompanied it, like a mixture of victory and loss. Oscar wasn't entirely sure what to make of it.

He sat up. Rubbed his head. He felt light, almost empty.

Then he realised he was in a place not of this world. Nor was it of Heaven, or of Hell.

In fact, he was fairly sure this was Purgatory.

He pushed himself to his knees, then pushed himself to his feet. He stood, rubbing his head.

A groan came from behind him.

He turned to see a creature on the floor. Curled up, gooey, in pain. Demonic in nature, yet somehow vulnerable.

"It's him," came a voice from behind Oscar that sparked a smile.

Oscar turned around to see Julian, a warm smile ready to greet him. At first, Oscar was wary, as Julian and he had not always seen eye to eye — but Julian seemed genuinely pleased to see him.

"Or," Julian continued, "should I say, it is the form he takes whilst in this place. I'd imagine, should he be granted passage back to Hell, his form will resume what it once was."

"Should he be granted passage back to Hell? You mean there is an option where he doesn't go back to Hell, and we could defeat The Devil once and for all?"

"We could. But I think it's unlikely."

"Unlikely? Why would it be unlikely?"

Julian smiled and placed a reassuring hand on Oscar's back.

"Walk with me," he said, and they began walking. The boxed room had somehow extended, and Oscar followed Julian.

"I'm proud of you," said Julian. "You let go of the attachments that held you to Earth, and there was nothing he could beat you with. There is no one else in the world who has done what you did. Derek didn't. Edward King didn't. And I didn't."

"It felt bad, letting go of April."

"See, that was not what you did — it wasn't about you letting go of April. It was the letting go of the rage that your attachment to April caused. The anger, the fury, the jealousy — all of this fuelled his power over you."

Oscar nodded. "So what about April then? Is she safe?"

Julian hesitated.

"Once again, Oscar, you have another unfair choice laid out before you."

"Please, no. I don't want to make another choice. I'm done choosing."

"You've already made the choice. I have no doubt what you will pick, and that is why you are such a remarkable man."

"I — I don't understand."

Julian paused, turned around, and looked at the remnants of The Devil moaning on the floor.

"You can end him right now," Derek said. "By refusing to grant his passage back to Hell."

"And I am meant to choose whether or not to do that? What kind of choice is that?"

"That is not the choice. Just remember, when I give you the choice — there will always be another ruler of Hell. There will be someone to take his place."

"So what is the choice?"

Julian turned back to Oscar. Oscar looked back at the man who had always criticised him, yet had always been there to lead — and, let's not forget, had been there to take April off the street and teach her who she was. They both owed so much to him.

"When I first met you, I thought you were an irritating little boy," Julian said. "I could see how scared you were. You were weak. But you also had such impressive power in you. And, well, just look at what a person you have become."

"What's the choice, Julian?"

Julian hesitated, appearing deep in thought, then appearing resolved. Oscar knew Julian did not want to place this choice on him, but it was why he was here. It was his purpose for returning to Purgatory.

"If The Devil is to stay here," Julian finally spoke, "his attachment to April will not be severed. She will die too."

Oscar could see where this was going.

"And for her to live?" he prompted.

"The only way to sever his connection to April is to send him back to Hell. The process of his return will require a removal from all things linking him to your world."

"So I save both The Devil and April, or I kill them both?"

"Precisely."

Oscar's head dropped. He looked to his feet, at first despondent, then angry. He wanted to kick something, but there was nothing to kick, so instead he screamed, then screamed again, his long wail of anger echoing around Purgatory.

"This is bullshit!" he said.

Julian did not reply.

"Why are these stupid decisions always up to me? I had to choose between the world and April before, I chose April, look what happened! And now you want me to make the same choice again?"

"Yes," Julian said. "And, like I said, this is what is remarkable. What I really admire about you."

"What?" Oscar spat. What could Julian possibly admire about Oscar in this situation?

"The fact that, after all you have been through, after all the repercussions, after finally winning the fight, after all the pain and suffering — you will make the same choice. You will pick April."

"And you admire that? I thought you said I was a foolish child and cost the world for what I did? And now you admire it?"

Julian placed a hand on Oscar's shoulder.

"I was wrong, Oscar. You were right. After all, if we are to let those we love die, then what are we fighting for?"

"And what about the right decision for the sake of the world?"

"I care more about April than I care about anything, and, I suppose, all I could ask for in the man she chooses to love, is that he chooses her — not only once, but again and again."

"And if The Devil tries to fight his way back? If he succeeds? If he leaves Hell and this all just starts over again?"

"Then there will be a future generation of Sensitives ready to put him right back."

Oscar looked at The Devil. At the remnants of the most powerful evil to ever reign terror upon his world or any other. Watched him squirm. Watched him in pain.

And, without saying a word, he chose April and returned to his world.

THEA BOOMED OUT HER PRAYER, BUT SHE NEEDN'T. IN A sudden, unexpected moment, every body of the possessed fell, writhing in pain, falling to their feet.

She watched over them, seeing some being freed, seeing some die — but seeing the demonic torment end either way.

A few demons remained powerful, stubbornly resisting their victim's release. Thea marched toward these demons, placing her hand on each of their heads and forcing the demons out of the body.

Hundreds of bodies lay unconscious on the floor. Soon, their eyes opened, and blinked as they shielded their eyes from the light. People looked around, as if awaking from a long sleep. They struggled to understand where they were, or what they were doing, and that confusion was in all the faces.

But they were free. They were liberated, and Thea knew that, somehow, Oscar had done it.

Some people stood, meandered away, returning to a family that would be grateful to see them.

Thea returned up the hill, her legs aching. She ignored the pain. It could wait.

When she reached the top of the hill, she met Henry's eyes. Never had she seen such an expression of relief. They embraced, and both knew it was over.

It did not stop there. All across the United Kingdom, the possessed were freed. With The Devil gone, the balance shifted once again, but this time in Heaven's favour — and Heaven did not waste time in freeing the subjects of torment.

A child in Devon stopped telling his mother she deserved to die, and instead begged her to free him from the ropes before embracing the woman who had endured so much.

A grandfather in Edinburgh awoke, vomited, then fell off the bed. His limbs hurt, but he was laughing. He could feel the carpet again. He could hear the rain on the window. He could feel his lungs inflate and deflate.

A mother released her family from the basement where she had trapped them, and begged for their forgiveness. They could not understand what had forced this loving woman to commit such a horrendous act, and with such strength — but they knew, as soon as they saw her face, it was over. She finally looked like herself again.

Across the world, this continued.

In the United States, a daughter strapped to the bed opened her eyes one day to look into the weeping mother cowering over her bed and say the words, "I love you, Mom."

Her mother cried, only this time, it was from relief. From a release of the torture she had spent the last year living through.

In South Africa, a man who had terrorised his village awoke and put it back together. He helped everyone he'd hurt, he restored every item he'd destroyed, and he apologised to everyone who had been dealing with the horrors the demon had forced him to commit.

In Iraq, a young girl awoke in time to stop herself from plummeting the sharp end of a knife into her father's eye.

In Denmark, a child was freed, a mother was liberated, a father was let go.

All over the world, in Europe, Africa, Asia, Australasia, South America, North America… People awoke.

People who had not been truly awake for a very long time.

Their senses returned, and they returned to what they once were.

The damage could never be undone. But the wars ended. Acts of genocide ceased. Individuals who had suffered the worst suddenly hoped for the best.

It all ended, yet it all begun.

And there were a few people responsible that the world would never know of and never thank.

But the Sensitives didn't need it.

They had finally brought the world back into balance.

And nobody needed to know.

A FEW DAYS LATER

OSCAR SAT AT THE KITCHEN TABLE AND KEPT GLANCING AT THE For-Sale sign outside.

Sure, this had been the house where he and April had fallen in love, but it was also the house where a demon child had torn them apart, where Julian had died, and where The Devil had tormented her.

Unfortunately, he would not be around to see this house be sold, or to see them move out.

His body felt beyond tired. It was hanging off his bones. His heart was beating slower, and his lungs felt sluggish. It would not last much longer.

Lorenzo sipped on his cup of tea. He looked over his shoulder at April, standing in the garden, enjoying the outdoors. Relishing the smell of the flowers.

She had never seemed to think about the smell of the flowers or the joy of their garden before. Now, she spent most days savouring every moment.

"Is she not going to come in?" Lorenzo asked.

"She isn't interested in the politics of the Church," Oscar

replied. "I think she wants a bit of a break from demons for a while. I think we could all do with a break."

"I suppose that's understandable."

"Why are you here?"

Oscar decided to be direct and to the point. He hadn't much time left, and he did not want to waste it talking to the man in charge of covering up the biggest disaster to ever face mankind.

"We require a debrief after such an incident," Lorenzo said.

"An incident. Is that what you're calling it?"

"I would also like to extend our gratitude to you, on behalf of all the Church."

It was so insincere that Oscar ignored it.

"Is there anything you would like to ask us?" Lorenzo said.

"Yes, there is something," Oscar said. "How are you planning to cover this one up?"

Lorenzo seemed hesitant to answer. Oscar was tempted to point out what they had sacrificed, but Lorenzo seemed deem Oscar worthy of knowing.

"We released a new strain of flu," Lorenzo said. "It has spread through the world and become a global pandemic. As a result, people have been made to isolate themselves in doors."

"You released an infection so that people wouldn't go out?"

"It seemed the best way to ensure people did not interact with others. The news has been so preoccupied with it, that we could cover up the amount of deaths occurring because of demonic activity relatively easily."

Oscar shook his head in disbelief. "You are something else."

"I suppose you will also want to know how long you have left? I mean, you are essentially a walking corpse."

Oscar snorted back a laugh. Lorenzo did not even attempt to be tactful. Then again, why bother trying to be tactful to a dying man — let alone a man who was already, technically, dead.

"I don't think I need you to tell me," Oscar said. "I know it's a matter of hours rather than days."

"We will pay for your funeral."

"Oh, how kind."

A moment of uncomfortable silence hung between them.

"Well, I'll be off," Lorenzo said, standing, aware that there was nothing else he could say or do to help the situation.

He left his cup of tea unfinished and put his coat on. He walked to the door, but paused, looking back.

"There is something I wonder," Lorenzo said.

"Oh yeah? What is that?"

"We at the church have speculated that, in the moments after you defeated The Devil, you were likely both taken back to Purgatory."

"That's pretty accurate."

"And, well — I also speculated that, should The Devil have been left in Purgatory, he would have surely died. He could not survive without Hell."

"I'd imagine not."

"Well, I was wondering — do you know what happened? I mean, did you see it? Did The Devil remain in Purgatory to die, or was he granted access back to Hell?"

Oscar watched April outside, picking up a lily and holding it to her nose. Her body had still yet to return to normal. It still bore the scars and the stretches. There were marks on the top of her head where The Devil's horns had started coming through. She ached, but, unlike Oscar's body, hers was slowly returning to full health.

She had life. That was the main thing.

"I guess we'll never know," said Oscar.

Lorenzo thought about this for a moment.

"Hm," he said, then left, leaving the house and their lives, hopefully forever.

59

Two comfortable garden chairs were placed in the garden. April sat in one, and Oscar in the other. They had both leant their chairs right back so they could stare at the clear night sky.

Above them, the stars shone in all their glory.

Oscar's hand and April's hand reached out from their seats, holding onto each other.

From the doorway of the kitchen, Thea watched. But she did not intrude. She was sad for what was going to happen, but she had said her goodbyes that afternoon. Now, it was night-time, and tonight belonged to April and Oscar.

The stars, despite their light, were not shining so brightly in Oscar's eyes. It was growing dark. The thudding of his heart was no longer a thud, but a gentle tap. It was slowing, getting ready to stop. Like a runner at the end of a race, who had torn through the tape and been declared the winner, but was now jogging slowly, warming down.

April's head lolled to the side and looked at Oscar.

Oscar did not look back. He continued to look up, despite his vision fading to blurs.

"Oscar?" April said.

Oscar did not hear much. He could tell there was talking, but it was muffled, like he was underwater.

"Oscar, can you hear me?"

She squeezed his hand. He turned his head toward her.

His eyelids drooped.

He was close.

"Thank you, Oscar," April said.

She did not know if he could hear her. In fact, she did not know if he was even aware that she was still there. But his eyes, lolling as they were, were still focussed on her.

She thought about all the things she might say to him, if she knew that he could still understand what she was saying.

She didn't want to express gratitude for simply saving her. She wanted to thank him for everything that came before. For never giving up. For entering her life. For falling in love with her and allowing her to be lucky enough to fall back in love.

Perhaps there would be some miracle in the next few minutes. Heaven would see what Oscar had given for them, what he had done in their name, the way he had saved the world, and they would be forgiving. Perhaps they would grant him a longer life, would restore his body, would tell him he deserved a second chance.

They would go on holiday, just them. Maybe somewhere in Devon, or the south of France. They would go to the countryside. Get a dog. Take it for walks in the afternoon, and on late evening strolls.

They would stop at a pub. Have pub food. Sit in the beer garden until it closed, then walk back to their Air B&B.

They would hold each other until they slept.

They would kiss each other when they awoke.

And then they would do it all over again.

She went to tell Oscar, to reveal these plans she had made,

the life she had imagined for them and the happiness they could share.

But, seeing as she didn't have time to say any of it, she summed it up with three perfect words.

"I love you."

Oscar's head dropped.

The grip of his hand loosened.

His body was empty.

April did all she could to hold in tears, and she wiped a few on her sleeve.

She kept her hand between Oscar's limp fingers until she couldn't bear to hold them any longer.

She sat up.

Placed a hand on Oscar's forehead, and moved it down to close his eyes.

She kissed him on the forehead and walked back inside.

60

APRIL WALKED INSIDE, AND THEA PUT HER ARM AROUND HER.

She forced a smile, albeit a teary one.

Lorenzo had left a number to call when Oscar's body was ready. Thea would call it in a moment. For now, she just wanted to be there for April the way April had always been there for her. To let her take a moment. To let her feel what she was feeling and know that it was okay to be upset.

"It's over," Thea said. "The war is finally over."

April chuckled a little at her naivety.

"It's never over."

"What do you mean?" Thea asked.

"We didn't defeat The Devil. We just sent him back to Hell."

April left Thea's embrace and put the kettle on.

"Let me," Thea said, taking the kettle from her. "You sit down."

April let Thea make the tea, but did not sit down. She stood, gazing out of the doorway, looking at Oscar's body for the last time.

Just one last glance, then they'd call the number, and he'd be gone.

Thea finished the cups of tea and took them into the living room. April followed.

She made the call to Lorenzo, then they sat in comfortable silence, sipping on their drinks.

But there was something Thea had to know. The right time or not, she didn't understand April's comment.

"If this isn't the end," Thea asked, "then what do we do when he comes back? What would we do if he tries again?"

April did not answer Thea straight away. She looked down, considering this question. It was a question she knew she'd have to answer, but she thought she'd have more time before she had to do so.

Feeling Thea's stare on her, she felt pressured to say something, so she asked herself — what would they do?

Then she changed the question to *what would Oscar do?*

And then the answer didn't seem so difficult.

She looked up at Thea, smiling at her warmly.

The more she thought about it, the more obvious her reply was.

"Then we stop him," she said.

A simple answer, and a true one at that.

They would stop him.

And, knowing Oscar was safe, away from the difficult world he had endured, she knew he would provide her all the strength she needed.

After all, they had the gift.

They were the world's defence against demons.

They were The Sensitives, and this was just the beginning of their story.

THE END

WHICH RICK WOOD SERIES WILL YOU START NEXT?

You could try...

The Cia Rose Apocalypse Series

Shutter House

Or the Jay Sullivan Thriller Series, which Rick writes under the pseudonym Ed Grace

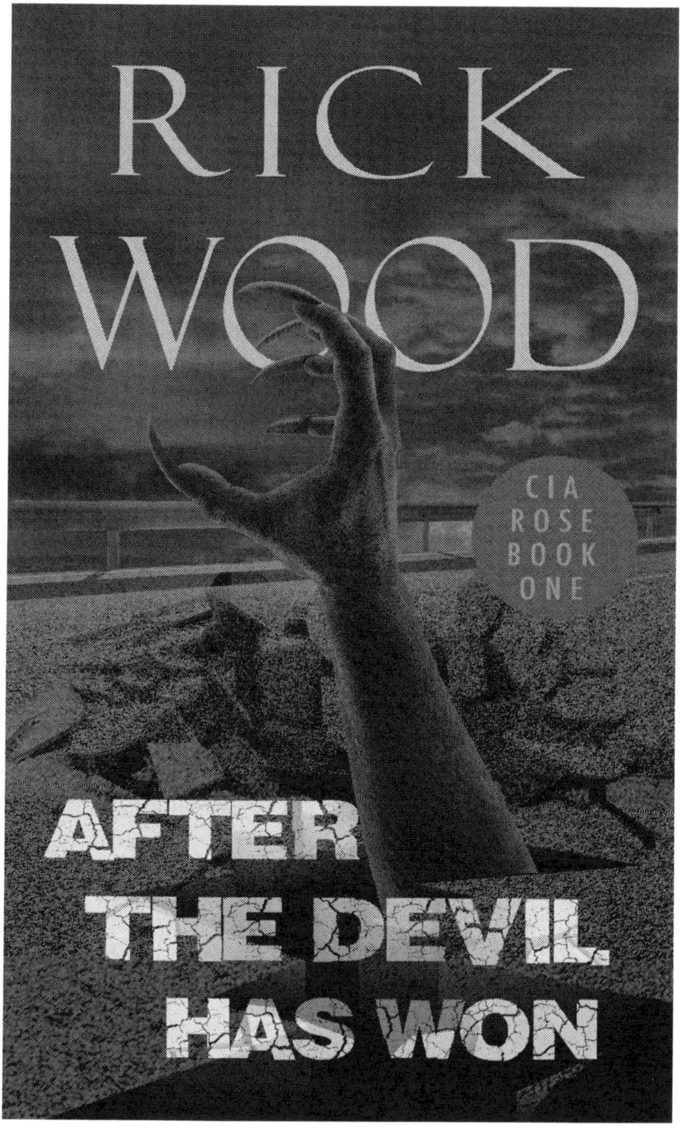
RICK WOOD
CIA ROSE BOOK ONE
AFTER THE DEVIL HAS WON

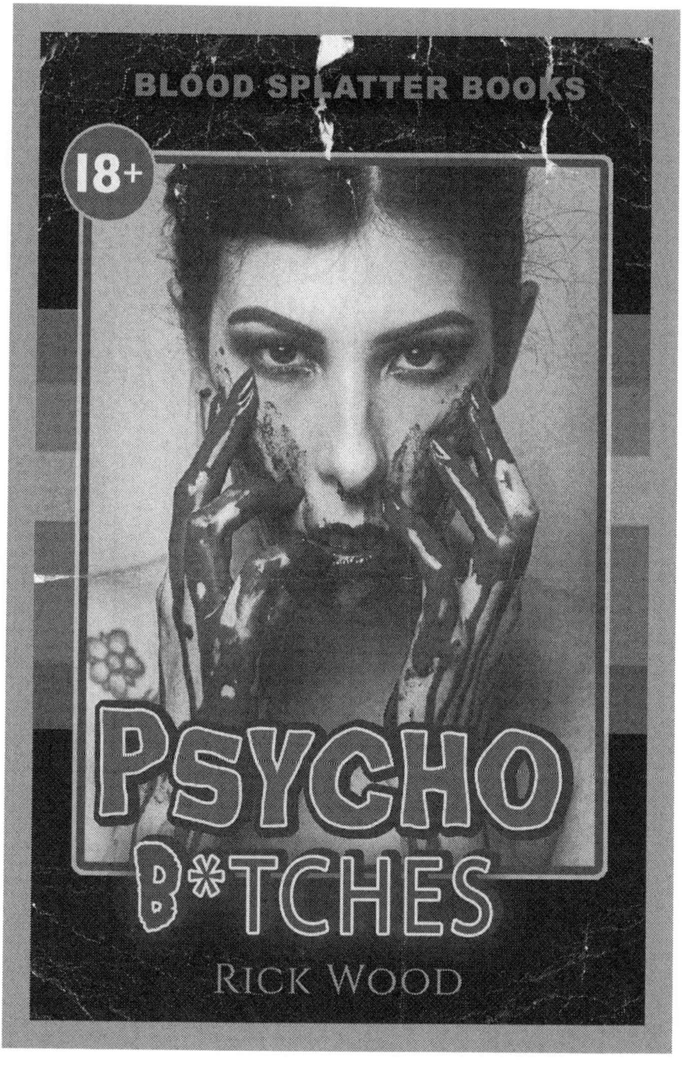
BLOOD SPLATTER BOOKS
18+
PSYCHO
B*TCHES
RICK WOOD

THIS BOOK IS FULL OF BODIES

RICK WOOD

ED GRACE

ASSASSIN DOWN

A Jay Sullivan Thriller

WOULD YOU LIKE TWO FREE BOOKS?

Join Rick's Reader's Group for your free and exclusive novella: **www.rickwoodwriter.com/sign-up**

Printed in Great Britain
by Amazon